TERRA
INSANUS

EDWARD
LEE

deadite
press

DEADITE PRESS
P.O. BOX 10065
PORTLAND, OR 97296
www.DEADITEPRESS.com

AN ERASERHEAD PRESS COMPANY
www.ERASERHEADPRESS.com

ISBN: 978-1-62105-190-9

CONTENTS

THE STICK WOMAN

"I certainly didn't become a millionaire by wasting my money, so why waste good money on toilet paper, hmm?" he'd told her that first night six years ago. "*You,* my dear, are my toilet paper now, and that's what you will continue to be unless you want me to kill your son."

Would he really do that? "No," Priscilla said. She didn't believe him. Even a sociopath like Fenton wouldn't kill their *only child.* And of the request he'd made? What kind of deranged person would want such a thing?

The answer came that same night, however, when her loving husband had piped down some video clips onto the television, one of hundreds she would have no choice but to catch glimpses of over the next half a decade. Snuff films, she guessed they were called. Homemade. Men in masks beating children, then raping them, then killing them. Priscilla felt certain one of the masked men was Fenton. *Anyone that... sick,* she realized, *must be capable of anything.*

"Okay." The word scratched out her throat, like a nail against stone. What could she do? Call his bluff? Ricky was all she had left in the world, even *this* world, this basement prison Fenton had consigned her to, this chamber of dementia that would make the Marquis de Sade hurl his lunch. "I'll do anything you say," Priscilla Brentworth had agreed the next day. "Just don't... hurt...our son."

Moments later, Fenton was bent over, his Italian slacks at his ankles. Priscilla's face wilted, but she did it, and she knew now she would always do it. *He'll kill our son. He'll kill Ricky. So do it! Do it!*

"Good, good, that's a good dutiful wife," Fenton chortled. "Nice and clean...."

***

A psychopath, but a rich one. Priscilla had discovered Fenton Collins Brentworth's pathological quirks only *after* her own

7

greed allowed her to marry him. *Too late,* she thought.

For fifteen years, she'd been his pretty piece of country club furniture, the ex-model socialite wife who'd given him a beautiful child. She could not account for Fenton's sickness, only snippets of an abnormal psych course she'd taken at Maryland. *Emblematic rectal fixations. Stage sociopathy. Transitive oral-analism with conative misogynistic-obsession-syndrome.* Fenton's perversion lay deeply rooted in a multi-faceted hatred of women, and by making her do this, the symbol was made flesh. Hence, her imprisonment in general, and the anal thing in specificity. One night, she'd merely awakened in the basement with a bump on her head. "I told everyone that you left me for another man, went back to your hometown." It was so flawlessly simple. With no living relatives, no friends to speak of? Who would inquire? Why would anyone suspect something so utterly depraved of a multi-millionaire loved by all?

The basement had a toilet, a 4K Ultra Sony 50-inch flat screen, and a chair. After the first year, the chair had been replaced with a *wheel*chair, to accommodate her sudden lack of feet. She'd tried to kick him one night. Big mistake. "Next time, I'll cut your hands off, darling. If you ever try to hurt me, ever again. And if you ever even so much a hesitate to tend to my need, I'll kill Richard. He's a freshman in college now, Princeton. Marvelous grades, just like his dear old dad." Over the years, Fenton would pipe down other video clips onto the TV : Richard's first car, Richard in a tux before the senior prom, Richard's high school graduation, etc. Priscilla wept.

"So," he'd clarified for her, "you will lick the feces off of my rectum whenever I desire you to."

"Why? Why?" she'd sobbed, convulsing. "Why are you doing this to me?"

"Why?" He'd chuckled. "Because I'm insane."

So here was Priscilla Brentworth's plight, in order to

keep her son alive. Two, three, even four times a day, Fenton would unlock the basement door, come down, and have a bowel movement in the toilet. Then he'd lean over, standing in front of the wheelchair, whereupon Priscilla would bury her face in his bulbous buttocks, licking him clean. And he had a knack for amusing little comments during her ministrations. "Sichuan Beef Proper last night. Can you taste the peppers?" or "Pardon the diarrhea, dear. I've been a little queasy of late." On feisty nights he'd haul her out of the chair and sodomize her, coming into her bowel and then instructing her to fellate him. "It's only proper you have a taste of your own on occasion." And sometimes he'd urinate into her bowel too, filling her up till she bloated. "Don't worry, darling. That was nearly an entire of bottle of Montrachet '57. I only piss the very *best* up *my* wife's ass." Afterward, of course, she'd struggle to the commode and void it all in a forceful, still-warm stream.

* * *

After so many years, her clothes had rotted, leaving her to sit naked in the wheelchair, mindlessly watching soap operas and talk shows. Once a Jerry Springer clone had hosted a coterie of adults who belonged to a "Diaper-Wearing" Organization. Yes, seemingly normal adults who would come home from their respectable jobs and then don diapers and sit in playpens with their spouses. "It's perfectly healthy," the club's chairman insisted. "It reattunes us to our childhoods, reformulates infant ideals to relieve the stress factors of adult life." "You're sick!" an audience member bellowed in reply. But all Priscilla could do was shake her head. *Buddy, if you think he's sick, you ought to meet my husband.*

9

***

The worst part, of course, was the taste of his excrement in her mouth. Semi-sweet, with a creamy sheen that lingered for hours. All she had to wash her mouth out with was toilet water since Fenton had deliberately neglected to supply her with a toothbrush, a sink, Listerine, etc. Priscilla's teeth had corroded to black, furry pebbles by the fourth year, each of which she'd spat out like malformed pills.

He fed her when he remembered, an opened can of spaghetti and a tumbler of water, generally twice a day. Every so often, however, he'd forget, sometimes for days such that, by now, her physicality had reverted to something akin to a living skeleton; less than ninety pounds, her head a skin-covered skull. The once ample breasts had shrunk to empty flaps of flesh. The lines between her ribs reminded her of death-camp footage, and her hair, long-since gray now, had grown to the floor. Clumps of hair under her arms, a clump of hair between her legs like a rat's nest, hair tracing her legs all the way to the bulbed stumps where her feet used to be. And not being able to bathe for six years only provided the finishing touches onto the horror show that was now her life. Her own smells appalled her. Every night she dreamed of herself in Bosch's Hell: a stick-figure cretin with jutting hipbones and fleshless buttocks, being eaten by beaked demons.

***

The television couldn't be turned off, nor could its volume be turned down, and anytime Fenton desired to sicken her further, he'd pipe down still more underground pornography. Images that beggared description and only increased her conviction that she had married quite possibly the most depraved person to ever live. One minute she'd be numbly watching *Big Bang Theory,* and the next it was some new excursion of disgust. *Where does he get these movies? And who makes them?* It was hard to imagine even the worst sort of human scum purveying such tapes, but then there was always Fenton himself proving the validity of the market.

Bestiality seemed a Fenton Brentworth favorite, some even complete with coy titles like *Makin' Bacon, Horsin' Around,* and *Dog Day Afternoon.* Here was another one called *Natal Attraction,* in which several men fornicated with a drug-gazed woman clearly late in her third trimester. Their intercourse grew so frenetic that eventually she broke her water. Men urinating on women, vomiting on them, inserting any conceivable object, including dead snakes, eels, and fish, into their rectums and vaginal barrels. More women, obviously drug addicts, chugging down goblets of urine, eating excrement with a spoon, shitting on each other as they twitched for their next fix. In one film, a woman extracted yeast and chlamyidiotic effusions from another woman's vagina, with a spoon, then ate the dollop of paste without a flinch, while yet another woman sucked pus from herpetic rectums and gonococcal penises with equal disregard. More films proved even worse: gang rapes, beatings, torture. Restrained women screamed bulge-eyed as long needles were calmly inserted into breasts, nipples, clitori, and even their open eyes. And of course, the aforementioned snuff movies. In one film a woman was skinned alive, in another rectal retractors were utilized to distend a woman's anus to a wide open whole; she screamed and vomited as hooks were inserted, her lower g.i. tract slowly but surely dragged out in pink loops. Women strangled, knifed, shot in the head, women forced to eat parts of themselves and eventually bleed to death via the wounds. In one film, a woman's head was cut off with a coping saw, whereupon some demented soul inserted his penis into the open esophagus, to copulate.

No, there was no end to the movies, and obviously no

end to the absolute evil of men.

And, just as seemingly, there was no end to Priscilla Brentworth's travail as a living host to that same evil.

***

It was not until late in the fourth year that he cut off her hands. She'd been watching some cop show, where a tactical officer had cited the dangers of human hands. "Only twenty-six pounds of pressure is required to break a human neck," he'd gone on in this supreme expertise. "I once saw a dealer take out a trooper's eye with a single swipe of the thumb. I once saw a tweeked up girl in an ER kill a doctor merely by slamming the heel of her hand upward into his nose. We're talking a one-hundred-pound junkie taking out a healthy man twice her size. The blow pushed the sinitic filament straight into the brain..."

This dissertation enthralled Priscilla—the hope of the damned, and she'd followed the good officer's advise to the letter, with all her might. But, alas, the faltering blow had only bloodied Fenton's nose. He'd said nothing, leaving the basement only to return a few moments later with some string and a hacksaw. Then he'd choked her unconscious. She awoke to find stumps at the ends of her arms, the bloodflow staid by tourniquets. Her hands, tossed into the corner next to her feet, decomposed to a state of mummification. Over time, she noted that the fingernails continued to grow minutely.

Eating came with much more difficulty now, but eventually, she learned to utilize her stumps with at least enough proficiency to keep from starving. She now had chopsticks instead of hands. Like an insect wielding its appendages, she would upend the spaghetti can with the nubs and shake out the contents, then eat it off the floor. Grasping the tumbler of water proved harder but she learned that too. A resilient woman, in other words, sheerly adaptable. The nodelike carpel bone on right wrist enabled her to change TV channels, and getting onto the toilet soon became nothing more than a little inconvenience.

Now she was a true stick woman: sticks for legs, sticks for arms, a death-camp scarecrow with skin white as a trout's belly.

And at least she noted a consolation. What else could he cut off without killing her?

"Ricky graduated from Princeton today," Fenton proudly announced as Priscilla rose from a starvation-induced unconsciousness. "I flew up for the ceremony—that's why I wasn't able to feed you for several days."

Like an animal, then, Priscilla jacked the spaghetti out of the can and sucked it off the floor. Fenton, next, had his expected bowel movement and turned his buttocks to her attentions. "God, I missed this," he informed her as she licked up the residue. Then he raped her, pissed voluminously up her vagina, and ejaculated in her hair. "And I have more good news, darling. Our son is officially engaged!"

Priscilla nearly passed out again as her husband hoisted up his suit pants and further enthused. "The DePiester girl, you know, from Potomac? You used to go to bridge club with her mother. They'll make a lovely couple, won't they? Soon we'll have grandchildren, honey! Isn't it marvelous?"

Tears burned Priscilla's eyes as she looked up at the grinning monster. Then she passed out again.

***

Every so often, Fenton would bring her what he referred to as "treats." Bums, vagabonds, homeless persons. He'd bring them down blind-folded, then show her to them. "A thousand dollars, just as I promised," Fenton would announce and give the money to the bum. They never said a word as they raped her right there on the floor, their bodies reeking, their skin pocked with all manner of sores, rashes, eczema, etc. All the while, Fenton stood aside, glee in his eyes as he watched the degradation. Performing fellatio proved the worst part, a stench like she could not imagine: sagging scrotums unwashed for years, foreskins heavy with smegma which dissolved on her tongue as she gagged. "Oh, don't be such a whiner, darling. A little dickcheese never hurt anyone. If you're good, maybe next time I'll bring some crackers to go with it." Her stumps askew, she'd lay paralyzed on the floor as they left, covered in atrocious glue-like sweat, flecks of crust, scabs, and dandruff, and drying semen. Once he'd brought in a vagabond whose penis was so large she felt gored. "I found him just for you, darling. Women always want the big dick. Well...here it is!"

Her rectum had bled for days.

***

Suicide was beyond her means. With what could she kill herself? Breaking the television screen was impossible; it was mounted in the wall and covered with Lexan. Drowning herself in the toilet, bashing her head on the floor in hopes of a hematoma? No, even in her hell, she couldn't bring herself to attempt it, for if he caught her, and she survived, her tortures would be worse. But deep down, even though she may not have been consciously aware, there was indeed some potential happenstance she was living for.

Fenton's death.

***

Another day with no food or water. Priscilla knelt at the toilet to drink, as the TV blared. In the water's reflection, she glimpsed her face, and her heart missed a beat when she realized that *she* was the creature looking back.

"—by U.N. estimates, at least another 10,000 Rwandan Tutsis reported murdered by militia members as they attempted to flee," a wooden-faced newscaster dryly recounted. Then, more news:

"—charged with forty-four counts of child abuse over the three years he served as pastor. Authorities claimed that Father Winherst would regularly molest the children in the confessional."

"—eventually found the one-week-old infant in the bag of the family's trash compactor."

There's evil everywhere, came Priscilla's harried thought. *And what kind of god can there be to allow all of this?*

"An angel came to me," a woman boasted tearily when Priscilla changed channels. "I saw her, standing right in front of me. She was all glowing in light and smiling, and she told me to that Sue Ann's cancer would disappear overnight. And it did! The next day the doctors MRI'd her, and it was all gone, as if it had never been there at all! There really are angels! There really are miracles!"

Angels? Miracles? *Not here,* Priscilla thought.

But when she changed the channel again, her gaze locked on the scene. An ambulance parked before a great posh outdoor display. A huge white cake, long tables draped in pink linen. Grim-faced men in tuxedos and over-dressed blueblood wives looking on. Two more looked on as well. A pretty girl in a white bridal dress. A tall, handsome young man whose worried face looked all-too-familiar. It was her son. It was Ricky.

EMTs rushed the stretcher to the ambulance.

On the stretcher lay Fenton.

"—a untimely tragedy as multi-millionaire Fenton Collins Brentworth, respected businessman and frequent donator to charity, collapsed of a heart attack during his son's wedding ceremony."

Priscilla stared dumbstruck. She thought of angels. She

thought of miracles. *If there really is a god,* she thought, *if there really are miracles...*

"—entworth's estranged wife, a beauty pageant queen and former model with the renowned Kinion Agency, could not be found for comment."

Please, die.... Please say that he died....

"Mr. Brentworth died while in transit to South County General Hospital. Services will be held—"

She didn't need to hear any more; her prayer had been answered, her miracle had arrived.

Priscilla's heart raged. *Someone will come to the house soon—Ricky, lawyers, auditors—someone. If I can get to the top of the stairs and pound on the door...they'll hear me...*

I'm...I'm...I'm...

Priscilla's skin prickled in something akin to new life.

I'm free.

***

It seemed like a week that she waited there, though it was only a day and a half in actuality. Time dripped like tallow. Her wrist-nubs had bled pushing the infernal chair's rubber wheels to the end of the malodorous room. On her forearms, then, she'd struggled up the stairs in the fashion of an inchworm, dragging hair-veiled, tinderlike legs behind her. Three times she'd had to repeat the trek, in order to drink from the toilet.

And she waited and waited, until....

Clicking sounds and a metallic *snap!* woke her from a throbbing sleep. The door was opening.

"Help! Help me!" she wailed as best she could, pounding her scuffed and bloodied nubs on the door face. "Let me out!"

In her zeal, though, in the rigors of this exciting and even angelic revitalization, she lost her balance, canted up on a hip, and—

"Oh, shit!"

—wobbled back and tumbled down the stairs.

Some god. Nevertheless, Priscilla could hack it, couldn't she? After being raped by vagabonds, pissed in, starved, and divorced of her extremities? Disallowed to bathe, forced to watch underground pornography, threatened with the murder of her only child, and coerced to lick fecal residue off her husband's rectum—for *six years?* Certainly, a spill down the stairs amounted to nothing compared to that.

She thumped down head over stumps to the bottom, groggily rearranged herself, and focused her sunken Dachau eyes up the flight of stairs. A timid, hesitant figure lingered—

"Help me!"

—then began to come down.

Then this person, this angel more resplendent than the Archangel Gabriel Himself, stepped into the fetid light. It was Ricky.

"Are...are you...are you all right?"

Priscilla crawled forward on wrist-nubs and knees, her matted hair shaking white flakes, her gut sucking. "Ricky!" came her parched scream. "I saw the wedding on the news, the heart attack! I know what I must look like but don't be afraid! It's me! It's your mother! Fenton cut off my hands and feet and has kept me down here naked for six years!"

The figure above her stood poised. "Ah, well...I know."

"You..." Priscilla swallowed her perplexion as surely as she swallowed so much feces, semen, smegma, urine, and—of course—spaghetti, in the past.

"Dad told me all about it," her son affirmed, "while we were upstairs watching the videos. Great stuff, huh? Especially the snuff. But I just want you to know that everything's fine."

Fine, she thought, staring as the dead might stare up out of a corpse-pit.

"Fine?"

Edward Lee

"I even came down here some nights, when you were asleep in your chair, to look at you. You really are very beautiful, Mother." Ricky then set down two opened cans of spaghetti. "Sorry you weren't fed for so long, complications, you know, with the wedding and Dad dying and all. Wendy's wonderful. Wendy DePiester? You remember her. You used to go to bridge club with her mother. She's so beautiful, Mother, and—well, I didn't tell Dad this but—she's already pregnant. You'll have a grandchild in eight months!"

The word burped from her soul. "Fine." Then two more words. "My. God."

"You'll do it, right?" Ricky politely inquired of his mother. "I mean, you know, if you don't, I'll have no choice but to kill the kid. I'd have to rape the baby to death and film it, to make you watch. You don't want me to do that, do you?"

Priscilla simultaneously vomited and shit bile when she saw what her beloved son was doing next.

He'd dropped his trousers, sat on the toilet, and was quite loudly moving his bowels.

Then he stood up and turned, leaned over, and spread his buttocks with his hands.

"You'll do it, right, Mother? Like you did for Dad?"

Priscilla, then, out of no other recourse but instinct, began to crawl forward on her nubs and knees. After all, she had the baby to think of now, didn't she? Yes, she crawled forward and began to lick.

SHIT-HOUSE

[-the final edit-]

"The world," the protagonist whispers to himself. It's a very intent whisper, and a focused one. He is gazing out the window. It's so black outside. Surreally black, like anthracite in bright light. He thinks of some Lovecraftian excrescence summoned by occult science. The blackness is all-pervading and unutterable. A luminous abyss—

Yes, I think. *The world.*

In your head, you hear Howard Devoto's greatest words: "This is forever, the final edit..."

[-delicate cutters-]

It's a song by Throwing Muses. Perhaps, one day, he'll start his own band and call them Throwing Up Muses, because that's how he feels most of the time, whenever he dares to look out his window. Music is a muse. Oh, Sisters of the Heavenly Spring, assist my verse and arm my prose, so to let the word be the mirror of the thing. Dante molested.

The protagonist has dreams based on music, like the stuff Shelley sent back in the old days, or all those Fields of the Nephilim and Skinny Puppy tapes that Hodge recorded for him. Delicate nightmares which proffer a vision that—oh, yeah!—he can really relate to. It's a cumulative process, you know. Music that taps the sewer pipe of his mind.

It's his sewer pipe, indeed, but it's not his shit that flows there. It's the world's.

Flesh melded to gray, stoic metal. Machine oil blood, ball-bearing joints, and metal-alloy bone. Time-drip iv bags droop to morphine/epinephrin needles genetically adhered to wormlike blue veins as the beat goes on...

The clanging industrial metal beat of the delicate cutters in his head, boring down deep into the brainpulp.

To get to the really good shit.

21

[-news around the world-]

A woman a former nurse in Rio de Janeiro knocked her ex-boyfriend out with sodium amobarbital when he awoke he was handcuffed to her bed she snipped his penis off with a pair of shingle shears injected him with Desoxyn so he wouldn't lose consciousness and then she cut the penis up into little pieces with a knife and fork and made him eat it piece by piece.

An interesting query at the very least...

What does raw cock taste like?

A heyday of cuisine!

Cock Fondue. Sweet and Sour Penis. Spicy Cajun Pecker Gumbo. Cold Poached Dick Tenders in Mustard-Sorrel Sauce. Osso Cocko.

***

A man in Seattle pretended to be elated when his wife announced she was pregnant when she was late in her third trimester two men pulled her out of her car at a mall drove her to a an empty office building that was scheduled to be knocked down they took her to the fourth floor and threw her down an elevator shaft then dropped cinderblocks on her belly until she miscarried and died.

The husband paid them $250 each for the job.

***

The Anne Arundel County Police will tell you that Davidsonville, Maryland, is "the best body dump" in the state.

***

A Florida man got a 25-year prison sentence for raping a 15-year-old girl and cutting her arms off at the elbows. The girl didn't die, so they couldn't charge him with murder.

He was released after 8 years for good behavior.

Not long after, he raped, then murdered, then raped another woman.

***

The Serbians killed close to 250,000 Bosnians and have raped, via military field order, over 60,000 women and children. Serbian guard squads that succeeded in impregnating detained Bosnian women receive commendations in writing and extra weekend passes. The Bosnians did the same thing to the Serbians for 400 years but that's besides the point, and this was all 20 years ago anyway. ISIS makes them all look like amateurs.

***

Trade deficit bedamned! Who says foreign countries don't buy U.S. goods? The Chilean Secret Police once used, specifically, Black and Decker power tools with which to torture "political" offenders.

It's a name you can trust. Black and Decker.

***

10,000 American children disappear every year and are never seen again.

[-pedophilia party. rockin'!-]

It's okay for a Democratic congressman to have sex with 16-year-old boys but—goddamn!—if a Republican congressman has sex with 16-year-old girls, there will be hell to pay!

***

In Nurnburg, Germany, you saw a porn flick where two German guys were having sex with 6-year-olds. They greased their foot- long penises up with Vaseline, then went to work.

Very gently, of course.

After all, child pornography was legal then.

***

According to an F.B.I. magazine that an ex-girlfriend gave you, there is an entity in America known as "The Circuit" which entails coded "mail-drops" and anonymous "points" through which child pornography videos are distributed to eager patrons. "Kp" and "kiddy" is what the feds call it. They're not sure but it may be as great as a half-billion-dollar-per-year industry, and nobody knows about it. They snatch kids and "turn" them, put them in "the show" until they get too old—like about 12—then make them work the street till they're about 18 and considered "beat." Then they sell the kids to Mexico, Saudi Arabia, and Japan.

***

Rocco "The Eye" Monstroni ran regional "point" for a Sicilian-based "crime-pyramid." Someone dropped dime on the fuck and he pleaded for Federal Witness Protection and Identity Reassignment in exchange for turning federal evidence. He spun like a top. He sang like my fuckin' green parakeet, and the feds buried half a dozen wise guys in the stone motel for life plus ninety-nine years.

After the trial, the federal prosecutor asked Monstroni: "How could you do it? How could you perpetrate child pornography?"

Monstroni glared and answered: "I didn't perpetrate nothin'. The sick slimebags who buy the shit—they're the ones who perpetrate it. If people want somethin', and they're willing to pay, then there's always gonna be someone who'll get it for 'em. Frankly, the shit made me sick."

Interesting point, though.

Good job, Americans. Real good job!

[-be all that you can be, in the army-]

"It tastes kind of like pork, when you cook it right. You grind it up and fry it, but always grind up some fat and wild onion with it," Sergeant E-5 Sand told the wide-eyed, awestruck, young recruit.

"When you're in the bush, and you're starving... You'll eat."

***

APERS (anti-personnel) also known as "Beehive," compliments of the U.S. Army Munitions Command. A 105 or 120mm tank projectile with selectable proximity fuse. The round contains 1500 "fleshettes" or barbs which are deliberately rusted, to incite latent blood poisoning. It's a shotgun shell fired out of a tank.

"Beehive, Westmore," Sergeant Sand recommends. "If you ever go into combat, load plenty of beehive in your ready rack. One cap will clear a crowded football field, no lie. We nailed gook kids to the trees a dime a dozen with beehihve."

***

Bravo 1/83, 3rd Brigade, 1st Armored Division, Erlangen, West Germany. I was in our battalion maintenance shed, hand-polishing lug wrenches because we had IG inspection

25

coming up. IG inspections are a bitch, let me tell you. So out on the pad an HE operator on an M88 crane was lifting a five-ton, 750 horse-power diesel engine out of a deadlined M60A1-series tank. The engine is suspended about seven feet in the air, and then some black batt mechanic walks under the engine to open the trans plug. A blue static premonitory chill runs up my spine as I'm standing in the shed, watching–*He's dead,* I think—and sure enough, the operator's hand slips, and that five-ton engine free falls right smack-dab on the black mechanic's head. In visual shock, I call the post medical unit, and while I'm on the phone, my platoon leader, some Johnny Brown-Bar West Point pussy motherfucker named H——, who's the commander of a armor platoon, mind you, but doesn't know the difference between a tank track and a race track, he barges into the company maintenance shed, and orders: "Goddam it, Westmore! What are you doing on the phone! Get your ass out there and hose that blood off the pad ASAP! We've got an IG in less than an hour! I'm not gonna blow an IG because you wanna waste time calling an ambulance for a dead nigger!"

[-the album of sergeant sand-]

You know it's all true, all the things he did...

Sand's victor, an M60-straight strangely with no bore-evacuator, backed up into a defensive position in the Vietnam jungle, a wooden stake jutting from the bustle rack. A severed human head on the end of the stake.

***

Sand's German girlfriend on her hands and knees, distending her anus to a round, empty hole the size of the top of a beer can, and Sand about to admit his fist.

***

Sand smiling in the jungle, holding up a prize. A human arm.

***

Sand smiling, sitting back on some crusty couch in a Saigon whorehouse. Other G.I.'s throwing U.S. dollar bills and MPC's like confetti while a South Vietnamese prostitute eats shit off the floor.

***

Sand's palms opened, displaying two human ears and what is probably a severed human penis.

***

Sand standing in the jungle with his arms crossed, looking down, and clearly waiting his turn, as an SSG copulates with the lower portion of a dead Vietnamese woman who had been cut in half at the waist when she tripped an M-18 Claymore anti-personnel mine.

***

Oh, yes. You know it's all true...

***

Because you saw the polaroids in Sergeant Sand's photo album.

[-oblique girl on the phone-]

27

"You don't believe everything you read, do you?" she asked on the phone that day when the light was silver and the tick of the clock was strangely loud, and she asked this with more venom in her voice than a coral snake's got in its poison ducts.

The relationship was ending.

"No," I answered in a voice like crumbling rocks. "But I sure as shit believe everything I see..."

[-seer-]

Such a fine line between that which serves as a blessing and that which serves as a curse.

I am a seer, you think, looking at the window.

And I...see...this...

[-the sound and the fury and the peep shows-]

The protagonist has always felt that he is a very visual person. Seeing fascinates him. He's a seer; he needs to see.

And the world has never been stingy with its sights.

The world, the protagonist thinks.

Such a visual world—

***

Doggone Days, Makin' Bacon, Horsin' Around: Women in sunglasses fucking dogs, blowing pigs, jerking off horses in barns. He saw them all, not surprisingly, in Baltimore. The pig bites one of the girls, and the other girls laugh. A German Shepherd frenetically humps a brunette who looks suspiciously like Martha Davis in The Motels. A dirty blonde frowns, beneath the potbellied horse, her hands jerking the lengthy pink rod until the copious release, into a plastic bag. After said release she upends the bag into her face.

New York, 8th Avenue & 42nd Street: Fat, mustachioed bald guy busts his fat, sausage-sized piss-hard-on into the blonde more beautiful than any woman the protagonist has ever seen in his life, all perfect, honest curves, noon-blue eyes, and white- blond hair shiny as silk. She is indefectible, paragonic. The guy sodomizes her so frenetically that at least an inch of her rectal vault prolapses with each stroke. Eventually, her rectum begins to bleed. Some time later, the man withdraws, ejaculates into her face, then wipes his bloody penis off in her lovely, silken blond hair.

Ron J. Extravaganza: Here he is, a kaleidoscope of sex with the same fat face, Ron J. slamming holes every which way, bending the gorgeous women in half, pushing their knees back to their ears, dog style, from behind, upside-down, one grueling flick after another. In one, Ron even blows himself— what a guy! And when the master is done he always obliges to charmingly release the seed of his loins into their faces or onto their backs, like someone taking a hock.

Ron Fuckin' J., yes sir. He sure knows how to treat a woman right—give yourself a slap on the back, Ron; it's a dirty job, but someone's gotta do it, so it might as well be you instead of someone with a life. This hair-matted, bulbous-bellied, indecorous slob's got it all, don't he? He gets to have constant sex with beautiful women, and...he gets paid for it. I read in the Adult Video Directory that Ron Jeremy has been in over 1000 x-rated films. Now that's what I call a real contribution to society.

If I ever see that disgusting, busted borsch-filled fat fuck on the street, I will throw the fuck up.

Poppin' Mamma: Two chuckling black guys with penises that look like things that should hang in a smokehouse take turns fornicating with a white woman who looks like about nine-and-a-half months pregnant. Eventually she breaks her water and passes out but the two guys masturbate into her hair anyway.

Champagne de Toilette: "I—I just can't help it!" she announces, stepping into the foyer. At once she lifts her skirt and urinates liberally on the floor. Washed out from a hundred dupes but still somehow glaringly sharp the blonde proves her diversity without a moment's hesitation, urinating into a big brandy snifter and gulping it right on down. "I just can't help it!" she reaffirms in a hot whine. Bright blue walls, like a Man From Uncle set, Aerosmith and Oingo Boingo playing from a boombox in the background. She couldn't possibly appear more appropriate: white high heels, black stockings, light pink blouse, dark-pink mini-skirt, black roots, smudged makeup—a real prize. She urinates steady streams into the air, douches with 7- Up, arranges herself on hands and knees and then expulses wine from her anus like a water cannon. Every so often the cameraman steps into the picture, pulls five-minute beer-pisses into her face and mouth, then ejaculates onto the side of her face. Then she's coming through the door, drops her purse on the floor, squats and urinates in the purse, then drinks from it. Next, she's in the bathroom, and what is she doing? She's inserting an entire banana into her vaginal barrel. When it's all the way in, she stands spread-legged over the open toilet and, by means of some very dextrous pelvic muscles, is ejecting the banana piece by piece into the toilet. Plunk, plunk, plunk, goes each piece. Then she gets down on her knees, licks the toilet rim, and begins to eat the banana pieces. Eventually the cameraman returns (hey, when a man's gotta go, a man's gotta go), holds her head down into the toilet, and pulls another five-minute beer-piss onto her head as she enthusiastically laps up toilet water.

Not exactly the kind of gal you'd want to bring home to meet mom and dad.

Boo-Boo's: The illustrious New York City again. In an hour of traversing this sick-fuck bung-hole of a city, I thought I'd seen everything, but, boy, was I wrong. I walked into a peep-show booth, and here's one called "Boo-Boo's." *What can this be?* I wonder as I drop in my tokens. Ah, people having sex but with a twist: all the participants possess some variation of at least one sexually transmitted disease. A pretty girl smiles, showing off the reddened bulbs of the oral herpes on her lips, while her erect suitor squeezes gonococcal pus out of his penis before he puts it in her mouth. When she's finished, another erection rages into the camera's view, the glans of which sports two marble-sized syphilitic knots. A fingernail breaks the crust off the pustules, and then the fellatio continues. Here's another girl opening her labia with her fingers for the camera, to display the thin white coat of chlamydiosis before yet another girl who lowers her tongue to probe the cheesy mess. And the final shot: a man is vigorously copulating with a sleek blond girl on what appears to be a kitchen table. He withdraws to ejaculate on her belly, then the camera zooms in for the revelatory close-up. The penis is so inflamed with herpetic boils it looks like a glistening, blood-red Pay Day. The girl leans forward to take it in her mouth, and I throw up before I can even get out of the stall.

Long Jean Silver: The woman's name is Jean, and she's about as cute as they come. The-Girl-Next-Door type of looks, honey- blonde, slim and trim, and a peaches-and-cream complexion. She was probably a cheerleader in high school. She's wearing a nice floral-patterned dress, fern-green, pretty. She quickly kneels before the other woman whose legs are thrust apart on the couch. Jean performs deft and thorough cunnilingus, and then—

Slicks her elegant, well-manicured hands up with some nameless lubricant until they shine like wet lacquer, and then—

Puts her oiled palms together and inserts both hands at once—that's right, both hands—into the other woman's vagina at the same time, until they're buried an inch past the wrists.

But is that all?

No, no, that's not all.

Jean stands up, sheds her pretty dress, and sits on the couch, chatting silently. Nude now, her beauty is even more apparent. Her flawless skin glows, her perfect blond hair seems to shimmer along with her smile. Her breasts, too, are perfect, not too small, not too large, high, firm 34B's. But—

There's something...

What the hell?

...wrong.

In time, the incongruence becomes noticeable. Jean's left leg is artificial. From the knee down, the flesh tone plastic shines garishly. And then Jean lifts her leg out of the prosthetic column.

What she withdraws is a long skin-covered bone. There is no foot on the end of it, just a tiny nub. Trace hair darkens the atrophied limb, which is also pocked by diminutive red sores.

She raises her thigh, wielding the emaciated lower leg dextrously, like an insect foreleg. Then she begins to slick it from knee to nub with the oil after which she unhesitantly inserts it into the other woman's vaginal cavity, to a depth of more than a foot.

***

Seen enough, seer?

Hmmm? Have you, seer?

***

But seeing is what he must always do. It is a curse. He is helpless.

He has to see.

He has to see what the world is.

[-west street whores-]

It never fails. Whenever the protagonist leaves the Ram's Head Tavern, the light at the hotel turns red, and out they come, like pus being effused from cankers in the night. A black pimp stops short, jumps out of his beat-to-shit Camaro, and hauls a white redneck girl by the hair into the car. His fist behind the windshield rises and falls for what seems minutes, and then the girl is thrown out of the car. She staggers away in a daze, her face beaten to pulp.

tap-tap-tap, a finger on the glass. The protagonist rolls down his passenger window one inch and a skinny white hooker grins in with broken teeth. "Fifteen bucks for head," she promises. "And no rubber. How about it? I'll suck your peter so hard your asshole'll inhale."

"Uh, no thanks," the protagonist replies, thinking, *Jesus Christ, is this light ever going to change!*

"All right, ten. Or maybe you wanna fuck me. Twenty to fuck me, and you ain't gotta use a rubber, either."

"Uh, no thanks."

"Come on, let's party. How about an ass-fuck? Forty bucks. You wanna ass-fuck me?"

"No. No, thank you."

"All right, I can tell. You want the special, huh?"

"Nnnnn," the protagonist begins, but then he stops. There he goes again, with his cursed curiosity. Suddenly, he has no choice. He has to ask.

"What's, uh, what's the special?"

"Usually I charge fifty, but for you . . . thirty-five, 'cos I can tell you're a nice guy. What I'll let you do, see, is you can fuck me up the ass, but before you come, you pull out, and then I'll suck you off. We call it the Shit Stick Special."

The protagonist's mind reels. He floors it through the red traffic light, and gets pulled over by a city cop at the next block.

[-pronouncement on a wall-]

"YOU KNOW THAT I WILL DO IT AND YOU DON'T GIVE A SHIT SO FUCK YOU BITCH, I'M NOT GONNA DO IT! DO IT TO YOURSELF INSTEAD."
(A graffito found on the wall of the ladies room in a New London, Connecticut bar, June 2002. It appeared to have been written in blood.)

[-1st street and 14th-]

A bum pisses himself in the Kojac's Sub Shop, gurgles phlegm, then dies as you're holding your half-eaten steak, egg, and cheese. A black woman taps at a vein in her corded elbow, then injects heroin whilst seated on a park bench as you and your pals stroll casually by. Mental invalids and epileptics jabber at you, rail convoluted obscenities from foaming mouths. In an alley behind the Roy Roger's, three teenagers chuckle as they urinate on a swaddled homeless woman trying to hide beneath cardboard. The city percolates, an asphalt abscess. In the stygian dark of Dave & Lee's Parking lot, a man is defecating on a car. On the corner by the liquor store there is a bloodstain shaped like West Virginia. A sound gets closer—WAP-WAP-WAP!—as you turn the corner. One man is hitting another man in the head with a two-by-four. WAP-WAP-WAP! Rats the size of puppies eat voraciously at a puddle of vomit by a dumpster. From the dumpster, a man emerges, rubbing his eyes. A short burst of machine-gun fire rings out, then a car speeds off. "Ice, Frog, Cokesmoke?" a black guy asks at the corner by Capital Books. "Tits, clits, and ice-cold Schlitz!" promises the barker in front of Benny's Rebel Room. "Seventeen tits, nine cunts, and nine assholes!" Another barker in front of a porn shack proudly announces, "Brand new films just in today, guys. Check 'em out. Fisting, shit-eating, animals.

We gotta great one where this really hot chick sticks sewing needles in her tits and squeezes out blood. Come on in and get your rocks off good."

And when you're finally leaving this abyss, this canyon of human refuse, the guy is still hitting the other guy in the head with the two-by-four.

WAP-WAP-WAP!

[-a sequence of graffiti-]

"Rippy sucks.
Rippy eats shit.
Who's Rippy?
I hate Rippy.
WHO THE FUCK IS RIPPY?
Rippy is dead. I killed him."
(A sequence of graffiti found in the men's room of a St. Pete Beach, Florida tavern.)

[-summation to a philosophical query-]

Every time I look out the fuckin' window I could just bend over and throw up, more from my heart than from my belly. Yeah, I'm a seer—what a joke! If I see one more thing—

If just one more crackhead tries to mug me, if one more bum tries to shake me down for cash, one more scrawny junkie hooker tries to hit me up for a trick, if one more sociopathic white-trash Maryland redneck motherfucker in a pickup truck tailgates me for driving the goddamn fucking speed limit...

Oh, I'm sorry, pardon me for being politically incorrect. Pardon me for being insensitive to others. Pardon me for ignoring the fact that I'm to blame for every whore and rummy and drug-addict and criminal and overall amotivate that all of history has produced. Pardon me for failing to realize that it's my fault every one's so fucked up.

Porn flicks, piss flicks, animal flicks, Long Jean Fuckin' Silver and her hairy skin-covered bone, herpes, AIDS, hepatitis-B, junkies, pimps, dealers on every corner, pederasts teaching junior high gym, daycare centers where they sodomize four-year-olds, skinheads with swastikas tattooed on their chests, evangelists busting virgins, United Way execs taking the Concord to have lunch in London, murderers sprung from the pen after doing three years, burglars bust into your house and when you shoot them, they sue you—and win. Liars, thieves, con men, everybody out for themselves and fuck everyone else, North American Man-Boy Love Associations, satanic churches where membership requires one ounce of your first-born's blood and KKK and L.A. riots and it's okay to rape and kill and loot because four asshole cops beat the shit out of some asshole with a mile-long rap sheet who was driving drunk a hundred miles per hour down a residential street and serial killers cooking biceps and crack addicts getting pregnant on purpose to get more welfare and gang bangs and nail parties and nerve gas and 5kt nuclear warheads the size of a can of Coke and people pissing and shitting in the fucking street and jacking out ninety-year-old ladies for their social security and then raping them to boot and S&M support groups and rehab for killers and Sex Addicts Anonymous and "fag-bashing," and gay Maryland congressmen who pick up sixteen year-old boys at night and vote against gay rights during the day and senators taking dope and writing call girls off on their taxes and judges taking graft and still more congressmen fucking kids and staying in office because it was only an "error in judgment" and lobbyists selling the country down the river and state legislation banning the dispensation of free condoms in high schools and the CIA buying heroin and log- rolling and deficits and cops on the take and nine-year-olds with MAC-10's and three-hundred-pound women in

Safeway using food stamps to buy better steaks than I've ever eaten in my life and still still still more congressmen missing votes in the house because they're out raking in honoraria at speaking engagements since they can't possibly live on $180,000 per year and newborn babies left in dumpsters and do-it-yourself abortion kits and how-to-make-two-step-explosive-devices-with-common-kitchen products manuals and psychopathic war vets and baby-stealing clubs and guys fucking pregnant girls till they break their water and killers for hire in the backs of magazines and hot shots and street gangs raping nuns and priests sodomizing boys in the confessional and death camps and rape camps and Shit Stick Specials...

So allow me now to unfold before you the summation of this inquirous philosophical manifest:

The world is a fucking shithouse.

[-the final edit-]

Yes, the Devoto song again. The protagonist is driving through the dank, rank, ever-familiar night. It has just rained; hence the black streets glitter like a strange, otherworldly frost. The State House dome glows blue in twilight, an azure skull. A redneck in a pickup truck tailgates him for driving the speed limit, and at the light a black kid spits on his car, and says, glaring, "White muv-fuck," like it's the protagonist's fault that the guy's ancestors were slaves, and then a hooker breathes "Fuck you" into his face with corpsepile breath when he informs her that he is not interested in her proposed exchange of currency for sexual services.

But now the protagonist shrugs and smiles. He's cool, he's together . . .

He looks out the windshield and thinks, *The world...*

In his trunk is a brand-new anodized Colt AR15A2 semi-automatic assault rifle with three forty-round clips and several hundred rounds of Winchester 5.56mm full-metal-jacket ammunition, not to mention a Zeiss low-light 3.5x scope.

Yes, the world is a shithouse, he acknowledges. *Am I'm going to start cleaning it up right now.*

Then the light turns green, and the protagonist drives on. It shouldn't take him too long to find a nice, dark alley where he can lock and load.

THE
USHERS

What...is *that?*

A figure in the dark?

Footsteps?

(-paramental entity-)

They are the protagonist's worst fear, his phobia incarnate.

The ushers.

His ultimate fear of going to hell.

Sometimes he thinks he can see them. In snatches, in glimpses. In hallucinogenic blinks and visual shivers. The pretty British girl in the Goth record store turns momentarily monstrous. That was twenty-five years ago, and there are no more record stores anymore because there are no more records. But you're pretty sure you just saw that same pretty British girl last week one a bus to Pinellas Park; she grinned at you with monster fangs. The figure in the dark, non-descript yet, somehow, disturbingly familiar. Or he'll glance into the next car at the traffic light, and the occupant will point at him with a fat, taloned hand.

Sometimes he sees them in his window at night . . .

***

What you fear most of all are the ushers. An abstraction, really—an aesthetic one.

After all, you're a horror novelist.

The ushers are spirits, they're ghosts. At least in this world they are. For there's another world where they are solid flesh and bone, all hot skin, teeth, and ageless

blood . . .

The ushers, you think.

An outland of your perceptivity, but rooted, of course, in your wasp faith, and your prevarication thereof. You put money in the Jerry Lewis jar and think that means you're a good person. You'll be on your way to the D.C. strip joints with your buddies and sometimes you'll give a bum a ten or a twenty.

You think that means you're going to heaven.

(-apparitions-)

He wanted to kill his father.

He came home from work one morning, trudging up the steps. He looks into his parents' bedroom and sees his father adjusting his tie in the mirror. "Hi, Lee," his father says.

His father has been dead since 1986.

***

You remember going to the hospital every day, watching your father's muscles turn to pudding, watching his brain turn to puree. Each day, you swear you're gonna bring your .38 to the fucking hospital and shoot the slack-armed thing in the railed bed, pop him quick in the head because you'd rather die yourself than bear any more witness to what nature is doing to him. Load up a Glaser Safety Slug, put the pillow over his face, and fire. Take your chances in court. If the shit-head Maryland judge sends you up to the joint, fine, then you'll pop yourself too. No big deal really. Life ain't *that* great, is it? A nightmare voice squalls a horror-movie voice distortion: "Hey, See-mo'! I'll beat myseff off wiff my hand affa I woke yo' ass. You MY bitch tonight!" No, you would not do well in such an environment. Better to be dead than a cellblock bitch. Fuck it.

***

"That's not my father!" he wants to scream at the nurse. "That *thing* is not my father!"

***

The night after he died—Christmas Night—he saw his father standing in the living room, draped in white sheets like something Dickensian.

Pointing with a bone-white finger.

```
(-nutty girl you picked up one night in
a bar-)
```

"One time I had an out-of-body experience. I went to this horrid black place, and when I woke up, I was covered with tiny flecks of wet hair. But the hair disappeared in a few minutes."

"Hmm. Flecks of hair. I think I've read about that."

"Do you believe in genetic memory?"

"I, uh—well..."

"I believe in psychical residuum. I believe in ghosts, I've seen them. Ghosts aren't always spirits of the dead, you know. Any kind of anguish, torture, or torment can leave a psychical stain."

"Psychical. Hmm."

"I mean, the person doesn't necessarily have to die. Why should they? The anguish is enough, to leave a ghost."

"Interesting, uh— Interesting point."

"Do you believe that you have lived before?"

"Gee, you know, I really don't think—"

"Do you believe that you can be haunted in *this* life by someone you murdered in a *past* life?"

```
(-midnight shift-)
```

Asleep in the Lodge, always the dutiful security guard. After a 6-Heineken buzz, and several videos–*The Bird With The Crystal Plumage, Three On A Meat-Hook,* oh, and, *Backside*

To The Future—you fall asleep and dream.

the eye of your dreaming mind is like a movie camera. you are the eye roving through untainted Maryland woodlands in the early 1700's of what is now St. Mary's County and Kent Island.

you are the killer. you are the destroyer.

you are the Conoye warlock . . .

women and children first, they're much more fun to rape and kill. the thunder of hoofs so dense it reminds you of the surf. you and your tribe unleash slaughter with impressive dexterity. great waves of dust unfurl in the wake of your hundred horses. screams unfurl too, bright beautiful screams, bright as sunlight. into blissful pandemonium you pour into the horde, encircling them as they try to flee. like threshers and scythes, the warhammers serenely rise and fall, felling arms, dividing skulls. one man is running away with a trade-ax in his head, brains shining pink in the newly formed cleft. another man runs off in the opposite direction, waving gushing stumps.

you've trapped them now, and cut them down like weeds. back and forth your squads of war-painted horsemen gallop over the dying and the dead, sewing blood and offal into the soil. then the dust abates, replaced by the wood-smoke of the pyres. the heavy aroma is intoxicating on the evening breeze, and you nourish yourself on the sapid and singularly savory meat, and fat around their liver, the wombs bursting with juice (and, sometimes, surprise nuggets), the ichor of their eyeballs...

a job well done, all in a day's work.

it's sacrifice, you know.

you are *sacrificing* the pale white intruder to the holy windigo of the forest.

here is our sacrifice!

hear our prayer, we beseech thee!

the few men left alive are systematically beheaded and dismembered. you stoop to dig out beating hearts with your flimsy trade-trowels, and squeeze the still-hot blood out of the meaty chambers, to drink. penises and scrotums are shorn out of groins. you use the scrotums for tobacco pouches, and after each raid you add a penis to the catgut war-necklace around your throat. your necklace, in fact, hosts more penises than any other member of the tribe. nearly one hundred.

the pregnant women are saved for last. you slice the milk-swollen breasts off a screaming pale thing whose belly is stretched pin-prick tight with child.

you sacrifice the gleaming child.

And wake up.

To see the two pallid-gray figures leaning over you. Faceless. Eyeless. One tall, one short.

They are both pointing at you.

***

A psychic ex-girlfriend who doesn't love him anymore told him in bed one night that she dreamed a strange man was in the room, leaning over. The man was showing her snapshots of a dead person.

"But it wasn't really a person," she queerly stated.

"What do you mean?"

"It was *half* a person. A woman, I think—everything from the waist up, like she'd been cut in half."

"Hmm. Strange."

"She was walking on her hands. She was walking on her hands...through a jungle."

***

And then there was always Aunt Annabelle. I woke up one night to a slow creaking. A rocking chair.

But there was no rocking chair in my room, there never had been. But here was Aunt Annabelle nonetheless, rocking away–*creak-creak-creak*—dead less than two days, and still shiny from mortician's makeup and formalin-based embalming fluid.

I could smell it.

"Aunt Annabelle?" I asked, leaning up in bed.

"Yes, it's me," she said.

"But you're—"

"I know."

With an eerie quickness, she stood up, and, yes, pointed at me...

"Do you remember Brad?" she asked, and was gone.

(-brad-)

Dougie and the fat kid were loping home from Summerset Elementary, down Shetland Lane. The fat kid was pissed because the day before, that asshole Donnie What'shisname had beaten him up, and he ran home crying. Thank God, he'd been alone then. No one had seen him cry.

A ways ahead of them, they could recognize the exclusive, wavering gait of Brad, toting his clumsy bookbag. Dougie and the fat kid were mad at Brad because he squealed on them to Miss Wendell, for throwing paper airplanes, so Dougie and the fat kid had to take notes home to their parents. Not good.

"Let's mess with Brad," Dougie enthused.

Anger burns in the fat kid's face. Not so much that Brad had gotten him in trouble but because that asshole Donnie What'shisname had made him cry yesterday.

"Okay," the fat kid agreed.

Brad walked funny, like a wooden marionette strung to the fingers of a drunk puppeteer.

Brad was crippled.

Dougie ran up from behind, like a Stuka descending, and snatched Brad's bookbag from his palsied hand. They jogged circles around Brad, right there on the corner of the fat kid's house. Brad wailed, almost fell...

Dougie and the fat kid were really laughing it up, tossing the bookbag back and forth over Brad's head. Brad's face puffed, the brink of tears, as he reached feebly at each toss.

"How do you like that, Brad?" Dougie laughed. "We're not giving it back. We're gonna throw it in the creek!"

"No!" Brad wailed.

"Come on!" the fat kid implored. "Let's really do it! Let's chuck it in the creek!" Then the fat kid paused a moment.

"Let's get him crying!"

Brad moved back and forth with all the finesse of a crab out of water, and he started crying forthwith. Dougie and the fat kid loved it!

A car came down the street, so they flung the bookbag over Brad's head and let it skitter across the asphalt. Brad, walking as though he had cinderblocks tied to his feet, picked it up and teetered home. Crying.

"See ya tomorrow, Baby Brad!" Dougie shouted.

"Yeah!" gusted the fat kid. "*Cry*baby!"

***

"Yeah, Aunt Annabelle," I whispered to the empty room, in tears. "I remember Brad."

(-haiku-)

You live alone. You
dial your number by mistake
and someone answers.

(-sergeant sand-)

"It tastes kind of like pork, when you cook it right. You grind

it up and fry it, but always grind up some fat and wild onion with it. Shit, when you're in the bush, and you're starving...
"You'll eat."

***

When I was in the Army, I was stationed in Ansbach, West Germany. This was back in the days when there was still an East and West. I was a tank gunner. Man, I could pick fucking cherries at 4000 meters. *Ba-BOOM!* The Army did a great job of turning high-school punks into homicidal machines—man, I *still* see HEAT and SABOT reticles in my head sometimes when I close my eyes, drawing a 105mm bead on a T-72. "Aim for the turret ring," my platoon leader always harped. "Then hit them with a HEP and spall the commie motherfuckers." HEP means High Explosive Plastic. What this round does is it impacts the side of the enemy turret, covers the turret with plastic explosive, then drives a delayed primer into the shit. Makes everything on the inside turret wall break off and cut the crew to ribbons at a velocity of about 1,200 feet per second. Popping caps, we called it, and these were big caps. I was such an asshole. I thought I wanted to kill Russians for my fucked-up country.

Truth is, they would've killed me first.

Anyway, there was a guy in my barrack named Sergeant Sand. That's right, Sand, like the shit at the beach. He was in The Nam. 11-Echo, tanker. Hell on fuckin' wheels, man. You put 'em up, we churn 'em up. We eat napalm for breakfast and piss transmission fluid. Grease our fuckin' treads with your 16-year-old girlfriends, man, and your mamas too, and your daddies. Hey, Ivan, where you wanna be buried after I pop your victor with enough HEAT to fill a fucking bathtub, huh? Roast Toasties, that's what we'll make ya. We'll rock your fuckin' commie world, man, oh man!

Anyway, this guy Sand, I thought he was cool. I

worshiped the guy. At 19, I thought that if I could be like anyone in the world, it would be Sergeant Sand. A one-man brass-ball battalion. A walking, talking world of fuckin' hurt.

He's dead now, or at least that's what I heard. He got TDY'd back to Fort Knox to train on the new M1A1's that came out in '82, 1500hp turbine engines, full main-gun stable. Turned out to be a piece of shit till they upgraded them to A-deuces. Anyway, I heard Sand got in bar fight one night in one of the "wet" counties of Kentucky, and got himself shot in the belly by some 'neck who thought Sand was putting the make on his wife. Knowing Sand, it was probably true. Oh, and it was a black guy did the job, which was karmic because Sand was an inveterate racist. But that's all beside the point.

Or maybe not.

Anyway, this guy Sand, he'd put cigarettes out on his tongue, then smile, then swallow. Killed Charlie Comm, lots of them, and had Polaroids to prove it. Said he'd get antsy if a week went by and he didn't kill anyone. In The Nam the 11-Echoes'd drive M60 straight series, and they'd roll through the jungle with severed heads on stakes sticking out of their bustle racks. Said he'd throw the Vietnamese kids moisture-activated fire pellets 'cos they'd pop 'em in their mouths thinking the shit was candy. Said he did a stint as a prison guard at Manheim, killed a guy who bit him on their way to transport, whapped the guy in the head so many times with his billy the guy's brains started coming out his ears. Sand had a German girlfriend who said her father was a gate guard for the SD at Belsen. "She can stand on her head and then lean over and go down on herself," Sand bragged, and it was true; I saw the Polaroids. "She's turned on by me 'cos I've killed guys," Sand claimed. "She used to be a whore at The Wall in Nurnberg, she'd do gang-bangs for forty marks per G.I." Sand said she could swallow twelve-inch knockwursts whole. Didn't believe it till he showed me the Polaroids.

Back to the story. This guy Sand, I used to party with him.

We'd drink these big bottles of Hofbrau, room temperature. For some reason when you're in Germany, the beer doesn't have to be cold. And, anyway, Sand's got this foot locker under his rack, and I ask him what's in it.

"You don't wanna know," he says. "You ain't got the belly for it."

"Come on, Sarge," I drunkenly plead. "What'cha got in that box?"

Sand gets up then. Looks at me with a face like it was carved out of rock. And he slides that locker out from under his rack and opens 'er up.

First thing he showed me was a bone. I dunno, two feet long or thereabouts. I looked at it real hard, but I was drunk, see? Took me a while to realize it was a human femur. Said he'd party in Saigon with the 176th MP's and these Navy SOG guys and Aussie Special Forces, they'd get a bunch of hookers together and pay them to eat shit. Didn't believe him till he showed me the Polaroids.

Pulled a jar out of the locker, had a baby's hand in it.

Pulled a leather bag out of the locker, full of human teeth.

Pulled out a crinkly wallet, made of skin.

Pulled out another bag full of scalps.

"Tell me a story, Sarge," I asked.

"Me and this guy named Winslow, we were on the same crew, he was TC, I was gunner. We didn't have SABOT in those days, we carried lots of HEAT and HEP, and BEEHIVE in the ready rack, and we also kept a few Willy Peter's around in case we had a gook bunker to paste. So we're on a road march one day real close to the safe end of Highway 13 and we blow our neutral safety switch, which, as you know, the fuckin' PAC won't run without. So we dial up maintenance on the AN and ask for help, figure those chuckheads'll dispatch a recovery vehicle which we were hoping. Those chuckheads would probably deadline the victor and we'd get to go back to the firebase and knock the bottom out of some whores' asses. Anyway, engineering batt says they've got an M88 on the way but it won't be there till morning, so we got a lot of time to kill and we're sittin' right smack-dab in the middle of some hot bush. So tell me what we did, kid."

"Set up a defensive perimeter?"

"Right. Draw the range card, line up the landmarks, haul on the cammie net, all that happy horseshit. And we're sitting there all day with our M-3's out, waiting to deal some serious lead poisoning to any dink who thinks he's gotta pair big enough to fuck with us, but nothing happens. So it gets dark, and we know we're shit for brains if we don't set up a hot line, so me and Winslow set up the Claymores around the site. You know how to lay Claymores, right?"

"Sure, Sarge. You kidding?" *FRONT TOWARDS ENEMY,* you think. "Can do it with my eyes closed."

"So anyway, we lay a hot line out. Most guys, they wouldn't bother, too much trouble, you know, but those guys are the chuckheads who always catch the MAC flight back to the World in a body bag. So me and Winslow, we sit in that hot bush all night hoping to get into the shit, and let me tell ya, you go out on a field problem in The Nam jungle for 20 days or so, and your OD's will *rot* right on your body, you pull your cock out to piss in the weeds and it stinks worse than a couple of dead Charlie Comm cooking in the bush for a few days, and bugs? Man, they had bugs over there that'd carry your mom away. Slugs with teeth, and fuckin' red fire ants big as your thumb. Lotta these ARVN guys were double agents; they'd walk off grid coordinates and wire 'em back to the VC arty crews. So we'd stake the fuckers naked to the ground, pour some sugar water on 'em, and, brother, those ants'd be eating their skin off in less time than it takes you to wipe your ass. They'd spin like tops, tell us anything we wanted to know, then we'd leave 'em there. And I swear they had spiders as big as fucking golf balls, and when those fuckers bit ya you were in the infirmary for a week."

But I'd heard all this shit before, from lots of guys. I wanted to hear about the hot line. "Come on, Sarge. Don't pull my dick."

Sand smiled, he knew. "Anyway, it was me and Winslow sitting up on watch. We had these two other guys on our victor, two niggers, Solkie and Buck—and I *swear*, the guy's name was Buck! But those two 'gers were cooping in the turret."

"Yeah, yeah," I said eagerly, "so it's you and Winslow on fire watch, waiting for the shit."

"Right. And we're sitting there with cocked M-3's, Winslow on the back deck, me on the front slope, dreaming about the World, about all the pussy we're gonna bust wide open, and how we're gonna drink enough beer to fill a fuckin' fuel gore, and then one of the Claymores gets tripped, like about 11 o'clock on the range card, and me and Winslow just about shit our OD's, 'cos you know what a Claymore sounds like going off. And we go check it out and find what it was that tripped the wire, some gook girl, probably 12 or so—dunno, maybe she was a sapper, or maybe just some kid prowling around, and what the Claymore did to her, she was like right on top of it when she tripped the fucker. Anyway, that Claymore cut this pan-face chick right in half..."

I was repulsed, yet simultaneously fascinated. Imagery, man. I've always been intrigued by imagery. And this was some image.

A girl cut in half.

"The two Jodys pop hatch, they're shit-scared," Sand went on. "They think it's Giap and the entire North Vietnamese Army coming down on their asses or something, or like maybe the fly boys off loaded a daisy-cutter by mistake, but we told 'em it was nothing, just a boar tripped the wire, so they go back down in the turret to coop. And me and Winslow are standing there with our M-3's, looking down at this mess. When I say this chick was cut in half, I mean like everything from the sternum up was lying face down in a puddle about ten yards away, arms out like a ref signaling a touchdown, and everything from the sternum down was laying right there at our feet."

Sergeant Sand paused then, cracked open another Hofbrau, lit a butt. Was this the end of the story?

"Well...yeah?" I asked, flummoxed. "What happened then?"

"We took turns fucking the lower half of the corpse," Sand said, and swigged his beer.

I stared at him, mortified.

No, no, I thought.

I didn't believe him.

Until he showed me the Polaroids.

***

Yeah. Back then I thought Sergeant Sand was cool. I wanted to *be* Sergeant Sand.

God forgive me.

`(-the ushers-)`

It is a fear-driven thing, these demented visions, these demonian ghosts born of the abyss in his own mind.

He often considers that he may be insane, or worse: premonitory.

Sometimes a week will go by and he'll dream of baseball scores and they're always right the next day. Sometimes he dreams of a beautiful Asian woman whispering numbers into his ear. One day she whispers "five three three four," and the next day he gets a freelance check for $5334. One day she whispers "one-five-one" and later his agent calls to report a three-book sale, and the time on the clock reads 1:51 p.m. One day she whispers "three-one-four," and then that night at work he responds to a gunshot call which turns out to be a suicide, but the address on the house is 314.

He's prone to absolutely ludicrous dreams, often involving cruise ships and conventions in preposterous places and grocery stores full of sex fantasies and bakeries full of french crullers and apple twists. He dreams of tidal waves and sinking ships and seafood markets, of lost loves and loves never to be asserted, all in the most unseemly locations. One time he dreams of an old woman who turns into a rotisserie chicken. For fuck's sake.

In late-November, he fell asleep on the Rte. 6 bus back from Chinatown—another bus crashed on the same route at the same time, killing several passengers—and dreamed about a girl he really likes a lot but never had the balls to tell her. Then the Asian woman's face appeared in the dream and whispered "She will hate you on Monday, she will hate you on Monday," and a week later—on a Monday—the girl he likes hates him.

Sometimes he knows when his friends will sell a story or a book.

Sometimes he sees auras.

***

That nutty girl he'd picked up in the bar that night. She'd said something else, hadn't she?

"If you create something in your mind, and if you think about it hard enough, you can make it real."

He thinks now of golems crafted of clay with his own hands. The maker destroyed by what he makes.

***

He gives them a scene in all of his books. The ushers.

It seems appropriate. After all, he's a horror novelist.

Pug faces on stout, corded necks. Flesh the feel and hue of riverbed clay, pit-nostrils and chisel slits for eyes. They are bulldog-like in a sense, with limbs of bloated, bundled muscles, squab hands, and sausage-fat fingers with talons on the end.

They are malefactors, adjuncts, myrmidons.

There's a black moon in a red sky, a veil, horrid and vast, refulgent with luminous fog, and a lake of steaming excrement. From fissures in the black rock, the pitiable naked horde is expulsed. A great black grackle flies overhead, its black-marble eyes gazing down in reverent delight. The horde is a mass of screaming bodies, terror incarnate, living chaos.

And from the steaming lake, the ushers arise to bull into the horde amid suboctave chuckles, their fat hands at once twisting arms and legs quickly out of sockets, wrenching heads off flexing necks, yanking whole spinal columns out of stretched open mouths. Fire gushes in the distance, greasy black smoke pours from cracks and rabbets in the vale's stone face. The smell in the air is so sweet: boiling excrement, human fat cooking over crackling flames. The ushers travail, complacent in their servitude—honored in the call of their duties. Stout, stiffened pinkies calmly squash eyeballs in howling faces. Skin is flensed from bare backs as easily as wall paper being peeled, ears, noses, lips, and fingers are bitten off and nibbled as tidbits. Talons swipe to lay open bellies, misshapen fists are thrust into rectums through which innards are extricated like tissue paper from a gift box. The ushers grunt and chuckle, plodding on, popping heads with malformed feet, inhaling blood, holding faces steadfastly down to drown in the tarn of bubbling shit whence they came.

Yes, it is a grand day in hell. An *eternal* day.

Monstrous penises rise in heady arousal, any available orifice plundered for carnal pleasure. Their luciferic seed spurts in endless, globular gouts–thick as marmalade—vesicles drained only to be immediately refilled for still more lusty revel. No registrant of this horde of the damned can be left out, and here there is no discrimination as to gender. Rectums are fastidiously plumbed, vaginas routed to the point of prolapsation, mouths jam-packed with veined members as long and stout as rolling pins, and uteri are set aside on hot rocks, to cook. Tender, pink brains are swallowed whole. Raw testicles are eaten like big jelly beans.

And when it's over, the ushers stand proud over the gorgeous carnage. Smiling ever faintly. Their bellies filled. Their groins slaked.

Yes, then it's over, only to begin again and again and again forever and ever, remuneration *in aeternum*, recompense without end. As the saying goes: Payback's a Bitch. Well yes siree, it most certainly is.

And one of the ushers steps forward then through the hot smoke of the jubilee, its black-slit eyes leveled, its forked tongue licking feces off its lips.

Its inhuman hand slowly rises, and its finger points...

(-talk show-)

An old woman with clown-orange hair claims that she's psychic. She predicts that Ross Perot will run for president and take 20% of the vote. Then she predicts that in 1993, a wave of genocide will explode in East Europe, that death camps and rape camps will reemerge. Some of the audience actually laughs at the absurdity.

She talks about crystals, about Kirlian Photography and remote viewing and OBE's and trance-channeling.

And ghosts.

"Our sins are ghosts, too. They always come back, and if you look closely enough, you can see them..."

(-the ghost, part I-)

That day. About 3 p.m. The writer was walking home from Treasure Island; he'd just been to Ricky T's to take notes for a restaurant review assignment. Neat place, comfy outside bar; cool, dark inside. They had fried pickles. The owner, whose name really was Ricky T., would die some years later. He had a heart attack while eating in a competitor's restaurant, God rest his soul. It's possibly a Sunday when the writer–notes compiled and complete–was walking home under the gorgeous blaze of Florida sun. In the Year of Our Lord, 2002.

He'd just missed the bus but walking was fine. M.R. James, and Lovecraft as well, were big-time pedestrians, walked miles per day, so if it was good enough for them, it was good enough for the writer. Perhaps some of their greatness might seep into his mediocrity. Or perhaps not.

His daydream strides took him all the way down Coquina Way, past a seemingly endless row of houses of stucco and those curved-tile shingles. A woman's voice drifts out from somewhere: "Hi, Lee..."

He turns, unable to locate the source of the voice.

"Yes. It's me."

Who? he thinks.

Still no source. Some of the houses were for sale and unoccupied; the writer squints as the dead windows, for some sign. The his heart jolts: did a pale shape, perhaps like that of a head, move ever so traceably in one of the windows?

No, no. It's just a curtain...

Then the voice resounds again, and he'd never be sure exactly what it–or she–said, but it could've been, "Tonight."

A further tiny movement snagged his eye: a pale shape, disturbingly head-like. It seemed to have blond hair.

The moment, and its inexplicable ethereal static, passes, leaving the writer to stand for a full minute more in the middle of the street. Squinting.

***

That night. About 4 a.m.

He drank a lot in those days, close to every night at the bar. But on the night in question, he'd been alcohol-free for a week or so...or perhaps less. Whatever the case, he would often ply this fact against other, grimmer possibilities, and suggest that alcohol hallucinosis proffered a low order of probability.

He awoke–such a wonderful cliche!–in grainy darkness infinitesimally tinged by moonlight. It was either an after-plume of dream or his deeply mauled imagination, but he sensed a soundless motion move across the foot of his bed just as some impetus had opened his eyes. The motion had the possession of a shape that could only have been that of a human being. A shortish, thin human being, and a lighter blur where the hair would be: blond hair.

His heart tripped as his eyes become capable of more clarity. The thin figure moved quickly but yet falteringly, head down, arms at its sides. But even in the shifting darkness he was sure he detected the sweep of a modest bosom, and an inexpressible yet undeniable feminine air.

The figure traversed the rest of the room and turned quickly into the bathroom where it was then submerged in utter darkness.

Fuck, the writer thought. Fear clogged his throat like too much peanut butter. *Some woman is in my fuckin' apartment, and she must've broken in because I KNOW I locked the front door...*

He seemed to rise from the bed in slow-motion–too afraid, yes, to go into the bathroom–and slipped out to the front room and kitchen. He clicked on the kitchen light because it as the closest switch. The room bloomed in sudden light, then went black again.

The bulb burned out! And it was one of those corkscrew

kind that were supposed to last five years!

He patted his hand against the wall, side-stepping right, then clicked on the living room light, though referring to this tiny cubby as a "living room" was farcical. Nevertheless, the light came on and stayed on, verifying his certainty that the front door was locked from the inside. The windows were all locked and unbroken.

Some chick in is my bathroom and I want to know how she got in, he thought in a building ire.

But did he really? Did he *really* want to know that?

He spent the next dismal ten minutes just standing there, working up the courage to walk boldly into his bathroom and see who was there. But it was fear, of course, that kept his feet cemented to the twenty-year-old shitty carpet. You see, there was no light in the bathroom; the fixture was broken, and he'd never gotten around to telling the landlord. And he had no flashlight. Additionally, the bedroom light–one of those clamp-on Wal Mart jobs–stood in the farthest corner of the bedroom, and he didn't want to think of what might reach out and grab him as he plunged through the darkness for the switch.

More miserable minutes ticked by (a "misery of doubt," to quote M.R. James) and then, seemingly without an engagement of his own will, he crossed the murky bedroom, turned right, entered the bathroom which was lit only by a trickle of moonlight, froze in place, stared with eyes that may as well have been lidless, and saw the ghost.

(-the neighbor has a dream-)

The bane of any writer is when non-writers ask the infernal question: "Hey, how's the writing coming along?" Jeez.

I was raking leaves decades ago in the front yard, a real pain in the ass. I had three book deadlines on my head, but I gotta blow off a day of writing to rake up and bag all these ridiculous leaves. Anyway, the guy across the street's got nothing better to do than jack his jaw, so he meanders over with a beer, and I roll my eyes even before he says: "Hey, how's the writing coming along?"

"Uh, all right, I guess."

"Oh, man, you'll love this," he said next, "seein' that you write all that horror stuff. Last night I had a dream that'd make your hair stand up. A real doozy."

"Oh, yeah?" I asked without much of a choice.

"Yeah, man. I dreamed I woke up in my own bed, and I hear footsteps outside. So I get up real quiet 'cos I don't wanna wake the wife. And, anyway, I look out my bedroom window, out into my front yard, and I see this army guy down on one knee, all dressed up for combat. He's got the paint on his face and branches sticking out of his helmet like he's in Vietnam or something and he's holding a rifle. And, get this—the guy's guts are half-hanging out 'cos someone had shot him in the belly."

I kind of raised a brow. "That's it? That's your dream?"

"Oh, no, man," my chatty neighbor laughed. "Not by a long shot. This army guy's kind of looking around, like he's scared, like he hears something. And then...*I* hear something too."

I wanted to groan. "What did you hear?"

"Well, more footsteps. Only they weren't as loud as his. Then all of a sudden he raises his rifle and starts shooting at someone coming around the side of my house,
but—you know how dreams are—"

Dreams, I thought.

"—sometimes things don't make no sense, and I guess that's why his rifle didn't make any noise when he was firing. I could see the muzzleflash, but—"

"No sound," I said.

"Right. And then this army guy with the belly full of bullets drops his rifle on the lawn and runs away down the street, screaming."

"Screaming?" I asked. "But I thought you couldn't hear anything."

"No, no, I meant I couldn't hear the guy's gun going off, but I could hear everything else, and this guy was screaming bloody murder."

I nodded. "Hmm. Pretty weird dream."

"Oh, but that's not all. After this army guy runs away—"

"Runs away screaming, with a belly full of bullets," I reminded him.

"Right, after he runs away screaming with a belly full of bullets, I finally see what he was shooting at."

"The footsteps you heard."

"Right, the footsteps coming around the side of my house."

It is then, presumably for effect, that my motormouth neighbor momentarily paused his story, looking at me with a wise grin.

I tied up the last pain in the ass bag of leaves and decided to accommodate him. "All right, who was it?"

"It was legs, man."

"*Legs?*" I ask.

"That's right. Legs. They looked like a girl's legs, kinda slim and pretty. But anyway, that's what I saw in the dream. Two legs walking across my front yard. And you know what they did then, these legs?"

By then I was feeling a bit sick. "The legs followed the army guy, right?"

"Well, no. That's what you'd *think* they were going to do. I mean, that would've made sense, but... You know how dreams are."

"Sure." I looked at him then, a light sweat breaking out on my forehead. "So what did they do then, these legs?"

"Here's the part you'll love!" my neighbor guffawed. "They didn't follow the army guy at all. Instead, the legs started walking across the street, to *your* house!" My neighbor, then, slapped me on the back. "Pretty weird dream, huh?"

"Yeah, man," I concurred. "Pretty weird dream..."

(-number nine one four-)

Time means nothing now... There's only one thing left to do, when the only person I care about in this whole fuckin' world is you. My blood sifts through ashes; all my muses are all dead, and your smile puts Glock 17 to my head. Little angel-eyes and a doomsday kiss. I'm Roquentin's pallid *La Nausée,* I'm Nelson Algren's crippled bliss. Solipsistic love but no more soul to sell. I guess I'm meant to stay here and smolder in this noon-blue, jubilant hell. The augurs all lied; the wasteland just gets bigger. I'll go ahead and put the gun in my mouth, but would you please pull the trigger?

(-butcher-)

The conventioneer rushes to ready himself; he's got a panel in forty-five minutes, and he wants to grab a beer first, with Dallas, in the hotel bar. Well, maybe two beers—panels make him a little nervous. He gets out of the shower, dries himself, hurries to the bedroom in the muffled hotel quiet.

A pregnant woman is lying on the clean Scotch-Guard carpet. Her clothes have been torn off in shreds, what appears to be an off-white bustle dress like the kind of stuff women wore hundreds of years ago, only now it's streaked bright-red with blood, and she has been butchered right there on the floor via a manner of demented expertise too diabolical to describe.

The conventioneer stands slack-jawed. The image is *teeming,* stark and clear and sharp as a bezel in its clarity. Then the conventioneer blinks and, of course, the image is gone.

But he remembers the last thing he saw:
The woman's face split by a Conoye warhammer.

(-homecoming-)

Ocean City, Maryland, 1991. Yeah, that's where you and your pals went for a week in late-July. You drank a bottle of Sapporo while driving your brand-new car across the Chesapeake Bay Bridge (or perhaps more than one bottle). A straight shot down Route 50, and you're there.

Party hearty, man! Partyin' on the beach! Bikini City every day, it's enough to drive you nuts! And drinking in the Green Turtle every night—what a commendable way to live!

You stayed at a high-rise called the Atlantis. It looked like something out of a Fritz Leiber story: tall and thin with gun-slit windows, a spire of drab-beige cement. One day you're sitting on the can—what a deserving place for creative enlightenment—and you get an idea for a novel that you're sure will make you a million. Little did you know then that the book would never sell.

On Thursday night you wake up at exactly 3:15 a.m. (Wasn't that the "cryptic" time from *Amityville Horror?* Over a decade later you would hear that the whole book and movie was bullshit.) Anyway, you can't sleep. You have this funny feeling you're being watched, so clichéd but so true. You go out onto the balcony in your underwear, sit down, light a cigarette. Forty-four floors up, you're sitting there totally alone. The sky is drab, the color of disconsolation. A storm is coming. At times you swear you can feel the building actually move, and from somewhere you hear a washed-out voice yell:

"Hey!"

To your left the waves crash but you can barely hear them because it's so windy. And to your right...

Another high-rise. Dark. Not one of its hundreds of

windows are lit. But by now your eyes have acclimated to the gloom. You're staring at the other building . . .

And you see someone.

The tiniest figure. It seems to be standing on the opposing balcony. Just... standing there.

It's so weird. You stand up, grab the binoculars someone had brought to scope the girls on the beach in their bikinis and sweat-shellacked cleavage and tart-fat cameltoe. You're leaning out over the steel rail, focusing on the figure.

It's a boy, a seven or eight years old. But not dressed in beach garb. He's wearing long pants, a long-sleeve shirt buttoned at the collar, big clunky shoes.

He's holding a bookbag, staring right back at you with a face bereft of eyes...

Then he hobbles away and disappears.

```
(-the railroad tracks at Ulmerton and
Lakeview, 10-31-2011-)
```

You wouldn't learn the story of the railroad tracks until much later, almost exactly seven months later, as a matter of fact. But you were taking your garbage to the waste-can at the bus stop because...who wants to pay garbage men? Dusk was just beginning to bleed into the horizon this Halloween night. You couldn't wait till it got fully dark and walk the neighborhood looking at decorations. Any other Halloween you'd be in a bar, drinking beer but you all but quit drinking a year ago Labor Day. Beer suddenly tasted like shit! (Well, except Sapporo. And, several years later, your beer of habit would become Tsingtao, which is actually still brewed in China, whereas Sapporo is brewed in Canada on a Japanese "license"–oh, but why do I encumber you with these useless and unfitting details!) Anyway, as you made your regular trek to the garbage at the #59 bus stop garbage can–as you crossed the train tracks–you glance to your right, to the perimeter about two hundred yards off, where you'd buried your ex-girlfriend's rabbit. It was a big ass rabbit and Kathy had put the poor bugger's corpse in the freezer so it wouldn't rot before you could get down to St. Pete to pick it up. You remember riding the bus back–the #4–and breaking into laughter in front of everyone because in your satchel were two orders of friend clams from the 4th Street Shrimp Store *and* a big-ass frozen bunny. You wondered if anyone, anyone in all of human history, had ever traveled similarly with these two things in their satchel. Anyway, you buried the rabbit about two hundred yards off Ulmerton, on the railroad tracks. And as you'd walked back, you could've *sworn* you heard footsteps pacing you from the thicket, and even forms that could've been faces grimacing at you out of the foliage. At one point, you think you even heard footsteps *running* after you as you neared the road.

But of course, there was nothing. It's all that M.R. James you read!

Anyway. Back to the train tracks. Halloween night. You stuff your garbage in the can, then head back home. All Hallow's approacheth. You can see camp fires in the woods along the tracks–bums, you know, junkies, drunks, oh, the compassion!–but you see them as witch-fires as lucifer's servants revel in preparations for sabbat conjurations. Just as your Wal Mart sneakers take you across the tracks, a voice calls out, distantly while also emphatically clear: "You there! Who are you?"

It seemed the oddest thing for someone to call out to a stranger. Or perhaps it *wasn't* a stranger because oddest of all is that the words were called out in your voice.

***

What is . . . *that?*

A figure in the dark?

Footsteps?
Is it me?
Or is it getting hot in here?

***

The novelist shuts his computer down. He just got it and he hates it. He hates having to own one because writing seemed much more real on a manual typewriter. There's something obscene about all that technology existing between his brain and the paper. Anyway, this is retrospective now: the early '90s.

Progress.

He lights a cigarette and polishes off a Heineken, then looks out the window.

It's a beautiful night.

He gets ready, listening to This Mortal Coil and The Teargarden, puts on heather-gray slacks, a Lord & Taylor shirt, decent shoes, then he leaves. He's walking down desolate M Street with his pals, gearing up for the D.C. beer-snob bars and strip joints.

"Hey, man?" comes a destitute voice. "Can you spare some change?"

A hooded bum is standing there, with an overcoat of rotten rags.

"Just a bit of change to help me out?"

"Sure," the novelist says. Why not? By then he'd sold thirteen novels, short stories out the ass, comic scripts; he even sold film options on two books! *Yeah, why not?* the novelist decides, and then, ever the generous Christian, he digs into his pocket to help this poor bum cop a bottle of hooch. He extracts a ten-dollar bill.

"Thank ya, man. God bless ya."

The bum reaches out. But he doesn't open his hand to take the money.

Instead he points.

The fat taloned finger points right into the novelist's face, and within the hood, the usher smiles, and in a voice like crumbling rock, it says:

"Your ass belongs to us..."

THE
SEA-SLOP
THING

When the going gets tough, June reflected with a wince, *the tough hijack a sausage from the deli counter.* Indeed, it had been a hectic day at the deli, taking orders, running the slicer, tabulating the scale, etc., yet never–even during peak store hours–did Zefowitz, her boss, ever see fit to give her help. *I can't do it all myself,* June often complained. *Nobody in this fuckin' shit-hole grocery store works but me!* which was true. But even the worst job in the world was better than no job.

When there was finally no line at the deli, June put up the BE BACK IN TEN MINUTES sign, secreted the aforementioned sausage under her apron, and scurried to the employee's restrooms. *Shit, I'm horny as fuck!* In a moment's time, the stall door was locked, her pants and panties were down, and the foot-long sausage was sliding quite vigorously in and out of her already-drenched womanhood. These moods hit her more often now that she'd hit 40–hormone changes, she'd read in *Cosmo,* the ultimate peak of the woman's sex drive–and being stuck in the deli 12 hours a day (and with no over-time since she was "on salary") left her little time or energy to pursue intercourse of a variety more normal than sticking sausages in herself, and even if she *had* the time and energy, there was not one single member of the male population of this redneck sinkhole of a town who June would touch with a 10-foot pole. Ex-con, drunks, life-long pot heads, guys with a dozen kids from a dozen different redneck tramps, guys who hadn't had jobs for most of their adult life, and guys with cars but who couldn't drive due to multiple DUI's. *No, thanks!* was June's resolve. *I'll stick to sausage!*

She'd previously been fantasizing of being taken hard and rough by some faceless man who was football-player-sized: 6'8", 350 pounds, all muscle, just hot and heavy right there on the deli floor. His rippled body would squash her mercilessly into the tiles as his hips hammered her loins with the endurance of a gas-powered sod-pounder. June, close to smothering, would quiver through one bomb-burst orgasm after another while the faceless muscle-rack greedily pounded on, until at last the reward of his lust arrived. Given that this phantom lover was much larger than the average man in physical stature, he too was much larger than average in genital dimensions–10 inches, 12 or thereabouts, with the girth of a brawny wrist; and the volume and number of spurts of his ejaculation shared this "much-larger-than-average" trait. To be eloquent, the purse of June's womanly pleasures was flooded with one warm, adoring gust of seed after another. To be less than eloquent, the massive phantom cock and balls filled her squirming pussy up with so much spunk, he could've been pumping it into her with a fireplace bellows.

Hence, it was the recollection of this fantasy that June now summoned: standing spread-legged in the grocery store toilet stall, pants and panties at the ankles, apron jacked up, and banging a prodigious sausage fervidly in and out of her sex. The sausage was still shrink-wrapped, of course, and for those interested in minutiae, it was specifically a Dietz & Watson Chorizo Sweet Sausage, 12 inches long. It would be appropriate to mention that June, at 5'1" tall and 95 pounds, very much qualified as "petite," but her vaginal depth did not correspond to this qualification. She knew she could take more than 12 inches but she'd never met a man close that size. Once she'd used a 14 inch zucchini, and even *that* had not reached "rock bottom." As for width, 2 inches barely cut it but would do in a pinch; 2 and a half (about the girth of a beer bottle) was better. She'd tried 3 inches once (a Boar's Head Genoa Salami) but that had been a wee bit too much. But this Dietz & Watson? At precisely 2 and five-eighths, it seemed *made* for her. *Now I know the PERFECT width for me!* she celebrated.

And so horny was she that moment, and so stuffed was her head with the fantasy of being used as a fuck-dummy by a faceless giant, that on the tenth penetration of the Chorizo, she came so hard she nearly fell over in the stall, and nearly shouted out loud.

Holy motherfucking SHIT! she thought, panting, and then she hissed through her teeth, standing on tiptoes, at the delicious post-orgasmic sensation of slowly withdrawing that big honker of a sausage.

It was just what she needed to take the edge off a tiring, thankless, and very tedious day. *Much better now!* She collected herself quickly, kept an ear out for the door when she washed off the sausage, then put it under her apron, and whisked back to the deli where, thankfully, no customers were waiting. She had just put the Dietz & Watson back in the front display case when she turned around–

–and froze.

Mr. Zefowitz was standing behind her, arms crossed over the bulbous belly that stretched his white dress shirt nearly to the point of popping its buttons.

"Uh, hi, Mr. Zefowitz," June said.

"You're fired," Mr. Zefowitz said.

June, not a passive personality, replied, "You can't fire me! Everyone else in this store is too STUPID to run this deli!"

"That's true, but I *can* fire you and I just have."

"What for!" June bellowed.

"For masturbating with store inventory," and then he walked to the case, removed the culprit sausage, and patted one end of it into his open hand. He smiled.

Embarrassment turned June's face beet red but it only took a moment for that embarrassment to transform to stark-raving rage. "You fat fuckin' pervert! You have a camera in the ladies room!"

"Not *a* camera, several," her boss remarked. "Security cameras, for your safety. Any old psycho could come in off the street, walk into there, and rape someone. Then we'd get sued, and we can't have that, can we?"

"Well you're sure as shit gonna get sued now! I'm takin' this shit to Channel 9!"

He put the sausage back (why not? It was shrink wrapped) curled an index finger at her, and beckoned her into the back room. "Come in here to see why that will *never* happen."

Veins beat at June's temples. She was grinding her teeth she was so mad. She followed him into the back room, then he closed the door, and when he turned back around...

...his penis was out of his pants.

"Why is your dick out of your pants?" she asked, seething.

"Well, it *has* to be for you to suck it," he said. He pulled on in a bit, then scooped out his testicles. "And you *will* suck it and you'll swallow *everything* that comes out of it, otherwise that security tape will be on the internet five minutes from now."

June stared. She was shaking, she was vibrating. Then–
Then–

She sighed long and despondently, got on her knees, and began to suck.

***

Fuck! Shit! Piss! This was the character of June's reflections once she got hope. *No fuckin' job! How can I pay the rent!* Her useless, tits-on-a-bull, dead-beat of an ex-husband would be bringing the kids home from summer camp in a week, and with the piss-ant child support he paid, she couldn't even get a decent amount of groceries.

She plopped down in the ancient arm chair, and would've cried if she'd been so mad. Perhaps some TV would take her mind off things.

But no.

The TV was broken.

I am so screwed, and all because I just HAD to stick that

sausage in my cooter...

At least it had been a good orgasm.

The taste of Mr. Zefowitz's sperm still buzzed in her mouth. *It's funny how sperm tastes worse when it comes out of the dick of someone you hate. Yeck!* She should've bitten it off, not that there was much to bite. Everything seemed to go wrong for June. *Just once,* she thought, *just ONCE, why can't something go right?*

Her cellphone rang, and before he answered it, she saw the text message saying that her pay-as-you-go card would expire in one day. *No job, and no money to renew my card. The hits just keep on coming.*

Then she answered the phone, expecting a bill collector. "Hello?"

"Hey, sweetheart!" a sly male voice answered. It was Fishy, probably her only friend in town. "How's the love of my life doing today?"

"I don't know, Fishy. What's his name?"

Fishy barked laughter. Everybody called him Fishy because, well, he worked the docks and smelled like fish. "That's my gal! Always good for a laugh. Say, you ready for some good news?"

"Fuckin'-A yes I'm ready for some good news," she said, ever the gentlewoman. "All I've had all day is *bad* news."

Fishy chuckled. "Yeah, I heard. You got canned from the deli 'cos Zefowitz caught ya stickin' a leg of lamb in your cookie."

Steam may very well have shot from June's ears. "It was a Chorizo sausage, not a leg of fuckin' lamb! And-and, it's not true! And where did you hear that?"

"Aw, hell, damn near everyone. Whole town's talkin' about it."

Fuck! Fuck-fuck-FUCK! June thought.

"Just don't you worry about that none'a that, Junie," Fishy consoled. "I'se bet every dang gal in this town has stuck all *kinds*'a things in themselves."

Now she was truly close to tears. What could be worse than this? She'd have to move. Everyone would be calling her Sausage Girl. "Come on, Fishy. I thought you said you had *good* news."

"Oh, yeah, that's right. You know ole Captain Kupjack, don't ya?"

June made a face. "Yeah. That perverted old drunk's been trying to get in my pants since I was ten. I'm serious. *Ten.*"

Fishy chuckled. "Yeah, he's a rascal, all right. Anyway, he just pulled into the dock on his 42-footer."

"Shit," June muttered. "I was hoping you were gonna tell me his boat sunk with him in it, that fuckin' old crustcake diaper sniper."

"You're something, Junie, you really are. Anyhow, like I was sayin', he just pulled in, been gone two weeks. Devil Reef, I heard, and he must've brought back one hell of a catch 'cos he was spendin' money like water at the bar. Picked up everyone's tab."

"That scumbag skin-flint never bought anyone anything. Ever," June observed.

"Well, he sure as hail did today, and he's *still* down there buyin' drinks. Oh, and he bought hisself a brand-new Cadillac ta boot."

This didn't sound right. "Unless he brought in 20,000 pounds of rockfish, he couldn't make enough profit to pay off his crew and then buy a Caddie. And rockfish is out of season right now."

"Well, funny ya mention it, about his crew, I mean. When he left he had four fellas with him, but when he come back today, he had none. Said he dropped his crew off on Kent Island 'fore he pulled in. Ain't no one work for him from Kent Island that *I* know of."

June's shoulders drooped. This sounded like a run-around. "Fishy, I don't give a fuck about Kupjack, his crew,

Kent Island or *nothin'*. All I care about is good news, and if you don't have any, I gotta go."

"Hold up there, little girl! Don't let your titties get tied in a knot," Fishy said. "Lemme git to the best part. So when I was in the bar drinkin' on Kupjack, he slams like his tenth shot of Wild Turkey and he come to me and say, 'I need my boat painted, inside and out, and there ain't no painters in this town worth of pinch of dog shit, not one, 'cept June."

"Bullshit," June said. "Last time I saw that stewed old perv, he pinched my butt, so I told him if he was the last man on earth and I was hornier than a jackal in heat, I'd hang myself before I'd fuck him, and if he ever touched me again, I'd cut his dick off and use it for fish bait."

"Wow," Fishy laughed, "that's sure sendin' a message! But I'm serious. He know you and I are friends, so he tells me to tell you he wants to hire you to paint his boat, and if you agree he'll give me $100 for a finder's fee."

June winced. "Are you shitting me?"

"Ain't nothin' but the truth, hon, and I sure could use that c-note."

"Well, you can forget it. I wouldn't work for that creepy two-bit little-girl's-bicycle-seat-sniffing old crock for *any* amount of money," and she took a sip of the cold, two-day-old coffee sitting next to her: the last coffee in the house.

"It's a two month job, Junie, and he'll pay fifty bucks an hour, cash, daily."

June spat the fetid coffee in a wide spray across the room, where it dotted her velvet Elvis portrait. "Tell him I'll take the job!" she gagged. Drunken fat old pervert or not, that much money would solve all of June's problems for the next year!

"Be crazy not to," Fishy said. "Just you meet Captain Kupjack tomorrow mornin' at the dockyard."

"You can bet your ass, Fishy! Thanks!"

When she hung up, she squealed in proverbial glee. *Fifty*

bucks an hour! Finally, something GOOD happened to me! Good, indeed. And perhaps *too* good to be true...

***

Bright and early next morning, June walked briskly through the dockyard, whistling, for some reason, the theme for *Sponge Bob*. She'd been a boat-painter for several years but quit after that time someone had dropped a Micky into her iced tea. She didn't know what had happened to her in the four hours she was unconscious, but her anus hurt for days. *Was probably Kupjack, the dirty prick,* she thought. Even so, for fifty an hour? She'd just have to keep a close eye on anything she drank. *Wow,* came the next thought. She was approaching Kupjack's slip when she spied a brand-new gold-colored Cadillac Seville. The gold paint job looked tacky but still, *That's probably sixty grand! Kupjack must've leased it, wants people to think he's a high roller.*

"Thar she is!" cracked a hoarse voice. Did June smell whiskey breath even at *this* distance? The disheveled, pear-shaped man leaned against the railing of his ancient piece-of-shit dock-shed-turned-office. Kupjack was as broken down as the shed, and as old. His distended liver made his stomach stick out like a woman nine-months pregnant, and the big bushy Talibanish beard covered a huge pink face that was benchmarked by a warped nose akin to a rotten strawberry. Lastly, and most ridiculously, he wore a crooked, white captain's hat with a life-preserver on it.

Then he rubbed his crotch through his canvas overalls.

Great, June thought. "Fishy said you had work for me."

"Aw, yeah," the old man crackled. "Just come back from Dunedin Reef with a hold full of Crackjaw eel, done sold the lot to the Japs for top dollar."

"I heard it was *Devil's* Reef. And Crackjaw eel? Isn't that *freshwater* eel?"

When Kupjack hitched in a pause, his man-tits jiggles. "Well, no, we *passed* Devil's Reef, I mean, and you're right, it were hagfish eel. I always confuse 'em see? Ugly buggers all look the same...I mean the *eel,* not the Japs. Then I drop my crew off St. Mary's Island, where I meet up with the Jap fish broker."

"I heard you dropped your crew off at *Kent* Island," June said.

This second challenge gave the fat drunk a jolt of annoyance. "Well, you done heard wrong, little lady, and that ain't neither here or there, and, yeah, I got work for ya. I need my boat painted inside and out, every square inch. Fifty bucks an hour, and it'll likely last all summer."

June couldn't help but ask, "What's the catch?"

"Catch?"

"Come on, Captain. You been trying to get in my pants for as long as I remember, and *nobody* pays fifty an hour to paint a boat. If that pay comes along with me being your nookie, then forget it."

Kupjack threw his old bearded fat face back and cackled like a witch. "Aw, girl, you're a riot, you are! 'Tis true, I was randy in my day , and gals followed my dick down the street like it was the Pied fuckin' Piper, and with *good reason.* But them days is gone. I'm old as Moses and fat as Buddha, and I'm so filled with liquor they won't even need ta embalm me when I die. Shee-it, if ya wanna know the truth, I can beat my dick like a red-headed step-son and I *still* can't get it hard enough to spit."

June sighed. "Actually, Captain, I *didn't* need to know the truth with that amount of detail."

"Believe you me, ain't nothin' I'd like more'n to bury my hardwood in gal's tail and hump till she come so hard her eyeballs switch sockets, but, no, I'se afraid it'd be easier fer me to shoot pool with a piece'a over-cooked spaghetti. And the diabetes just make it worse." The old saltly dog lifted one leg, pulled up a pant cuff, and displayed a discolored ankle close to 6 inches thick. "Damn shit make my ankles get all swole up big around as a Russard Liverwurst, and that keeps the dick down too. Say, speakin' of liverwurst, is it true what I heard? That you got up'n fired from the deli for jack-hammerin' a liverwurst in and out'a your joy-trail?"

"No!" June exploded. "It's NOT!"

Kupjack shrugged lackadaisically. "Nothin' ta be 'shamed of, hon. Woman got every right to stick *anything she want* in her sauce-box, whether it be a liverwurst, a french bread, a bowling pin, one'a them big rolls'a cookie dough, a rotisserie pork roast–"

"I get the picture!" June yelled, her face turning evermore pink.

"Anyway, sweetie, the paint's on the deck'n boat's unlocked, start right away if ya like. You need anything"–he jerked a thumb backwards–"I'll be in the bar."

That's it? Just like that, I've got a fifty-buck-an-hour job? It seemed so.

"Uh, thanks, Captain."

"Shore thing, sugar," he said, limping down the ramp. "Oh, I forgot. Do below decks first, 'cos I ain't picked up the exterior paint yet, plus I gotta get my hoist repaired," and then he hobbled toward the bar.

June walked down to the slip where the 42-foot *Gwendylyn Rose* was docked, an old rattletrap but still chugging after decades. A pyramid of one-gallon paint cans sat stacked before the gang-ladder. All the supplies she'd need were right there as well, in a stationary storage locker. There was no time like the present so she pried the lid off a can, squatted down, and began to stir. Her first coherent thought to herself was a familiar one: *Shit, I'm horny as fuck!* June's sudden good fortune put her in a great mood, and when she was in a great mood...the juices got to flowing. *I must be a sex-maniac,* she concluded, and her sex already damp, *even though I never have sex with anything but vibrators, sausages, and vegetables.* The paint, epoxy-based, was hard to stir, yet the exertion didn't consciously occur to her. *I'm an orgasm addict, I guess,* and she supposed their were worse things to be. The position of her squat pressed the crotch of her cut-offs firm against her already throbbing pubis. *What I wouldn't give for a man right now, a great big fuckin' HUNK of a man with a dick the size of a baby's leg and balls like duck eggs.* Yes, something like that sliding into her and banging in and out like a bilge-pump piston would be just what the doctor ordered. So dense was this desire that she felt very tempted to take a break, go below decks, and give her "honey pot" a work-over. She could get her fist in there no problem, and only a few twists would be required to set off a powder-keg orgasm. *But, no, with my luck someone would see...* And that would be even worse than her previous humiliation at the deli.

She got back to stirring, and–

Oh, fuck. Not again.

That *Cosmo* article wasn't kidding about fortyish women. Her hormones must be overflowing, for her squat and the continued pressure of the crotch of her of shorts pressing again her "secret garden" continued to titillate her. Again she mused of her phantom suitor, the faceless armature of over-muscular flesh, legs wide and hard as railroad ties, and dinner-plate-sized hands manipulating her like a sack of packing peanuts, flinging off her top, hauling off her shorts and laying her out on her belly like a specimen. Her butt-cheeks were parted, then–

Kurrrrrrr-HOCK!

–a golf-ball-sized wad of spit landed right on her anus. *No, not there!* she thought. *No, not there!*

Her mental plea was answered by the prompt insertion of that perfect, throbbing, heavily veined tennis-ball-can-sized cock. June's cheeks billowed; just the first thrust squashed

the wind out of her. But once the mindless rhythm got going–
Yes, there! she thought. *Yes, there!*

Indeed, it felt like a *arm* going right up her butt. Was it actually prodding the bottom on her stomach? It occurred to June, in this peculiar moment of abstraction, that sometimes what a woman wanted more than anything was simply to be *filled,* to be used as a container of flesh and be *crammed* to the top, to be *stuffed* like a turkey until there was no more room to stuff anything more.

And if that's what women really wanted, that's what June was getting in the midst of this sopping, cringing, nerve-suckling fantasy.

Her heady glee could only be reflected by one word: *Fuck!*

The prodigious erection pistoned in an out, and the fact that it did so with *no regard for her at all* only made it more delicious. Her suitor's need had denuded her of all identity: she was no longer a thinking, living American woman, she was a squirming, flinching, mindless *thing* that was taken to be used solely as a receptacle for the phantom's animal lust.

And that was just fine with June! *My butt's being plungered like a gas station toilet...and I LOVE it!*

The phantom must've weighed 400 pounds, and all of it was muscle, and when it lay down flat it squashed June like Twinkie under cinder block (if he'd been filled with cream, like a Twinkie, it would be all over the place now!) All her breath was vised out of her; her tongue jutted. Every ounce of strength was required to wedge her hand under her belly and inch it toward her steaming sex, and she knew all it would take was a single press of her fingertip against her gorged clitoris and that would be that: Orgasm City.

Still, the brainless suitor humped her butt without relent. June's finger was two inches away, one inch, a half-inch–
Almost, almost...
–and just as the contact she craved would be achieved...

"Hey, girl, I say that's one mighty fine tail you'se stickin' out there!"

The marauding voice shattered the fantasy, and the gates to Orgasm City were slammed shut.

Shit! Who the–

June, transported back to the dull reality of her life in general and the even duller task of stirring a gallon of marine paint on the foredeck of this old rattletrap fishing boat, fired her glare behind her and down.

It was Rummy, the neighborhood dock bum, grinning toothless through a rust-colored beard that encompassed most of his face and scratching the crotch of dungarees that probably hadn't been washed in a year.

"It's rude to stare at people, Rummy!" she yelled.

"Gal with a butt like that make it hard not too, ummhmm! Look like you had somethin' naughty goin' on in yer head, the ways you was squirmin' and moanin' and–"

"As a matter of fact I did, and you just ruined it!" she barked and kept stirring.

"Well then what say you'n me go below decks and pick up where ya left off?"

What say you drink your own piss instead, June thought in a rage. "What do you want, Rummy?"

"'Sides you? Nothin', girl. Only I wanted ta ask if you heard 'bout Kupjack, but I guess ya have, seein' how you're workin' for him now."

"Brilliant observation, and, yeah, I heard he was back in town."

"Naw, naw, that ain't what I meant. I meant about Kelly Point."

June grimaced, stirring away. The paint was like taffy. "What about Kelly Point?"

When Rummy scratched his beard, a snowstorm of dandruff fell. "Well, accordin' to the local talk, that be where Kupjack just come back from, then he drop his crew off on Brewer Island. But when he pulls in here there weren't *nothin'* in his hold. Was *bone-dry's* what the dockmaster say. Then Kupjack up'n pay cash for that new Caddy and start spendin' money like Donald Strump...or whatever his name is. Donald Gates?"

June stopped stirring and whipped around. "Wait a minute. First I heard is was Devil's Reef, then Dunedin Reef, and now you're telling me he just came back from Kelly Point, and that he dropped his crew off a Brewer Island. Well, I heard it was St. Mary's Island after I heard it was Kent Island. What the hell's going on?"

"Gold, that's what."

June looked at him cockeyed. "Say again?"

"That's what I heard my own self...'twas *gold* he come back with, and it must've been a fair amount 'cos he walked out of the gold exchange in Salisbury this morning with a hundred grand, *cash.*"

June frowned. "Even if that's true, Rummy, how would you know?"

The man patted dust off his corroded shirt. "Simple. My sister works there. She told me."

In a town like this, June knew that most every bit of information communicated amongst the local population was ninety-nine-percent grapevine. "Fine, Rummy, but I still don't believe it."

"Then where'd Kupjack get the money?"

It's a good question, but... "I don't care," she resolved, then squatted back down to her stirring.

"And where *is* everybody?" Rummy continued the conjecture. The question was followed by a tinkling sound.

"What do you mean, where is—" but then June winced. Rummy was standing right there on the dockwalk in broad daylight, urinating into the water. "At least turn around when you do that, Rummy!"

"Oh, shee-it, sorry," he said. Were flies actually buzzing

around his exposed penis? He put it away but, without surprise, didn't even pull his zipper up. "Look around. Notice anything strange about the marina?"

It took June several moments to blink away the vision of Rummy's unwashed-for-years dick. But then, as her eyes surveyed the long expanse of boat-slips...

Damn near every boat is GONE... "Where'd everyone go?"

"Where you think?" Rummy replied. "They all high-tailed it to Kelly Point, to look for that stash of gold Kupjack found. Probably a lot more there." Rummy stepped down off the dock, into a small dingy, which was where he usually slept. "'S'where I'm a-goin' now, I ain't no dummy. You wanna come with me?" he added with a crack of enthusiasm.

"No," she said. "No, thank you."

"All's right then. See ya later."

Hope not, June thought at her cynical best. Rummy pulled a cord, started a small outboard motor, and puttered out to the bay.

This is some weird shit going on here, she thought. Devil's Reef, Dunedin Reef, Kelly Point, Kent Island, St. Mary's Island, crackjaw, hagfish, etc. *Every time I heard one thing, I hear another thing completely different. And...*

She stared at the thought. *Gold?*

She'd never heard of one speck of gold in these parts, ever. But it *was* odd about Kupjack's sudden spending spree. The only thing tighter than Kupjack's wallet was a bull's ass in fly season. And now that she thought of it, why would he have bought a gold Cadillac, of all colors? It looked like shit.

Salty sea-foam towns like this all had their local legends, but the subject of gold did not fit into any of them. No hidden treasure, no pirates, not sunken Spanish galleons.

The paint was stirred, and the sun was cooking her back. She lugged the can down to the companionway steps to the first cabin. Her mind kept swimming in questions as she opened the port-holes to get some cross-breeze. *Wouldn't it be funny as shit if I found a gold coin down here?* Then–

"Oww!"

In a split second, she'd stepped on something and fallen–*thunk!*–right on her butt. She'd need to get some lights on down here; it was too dark, and...

What did I trip over?

She squinted, patting her hand around on the floor. There was nothing–No! Her hand landed on something cool, hard, and irregular. Was it a piece of glazed porcelain? It felt smooth, polished.

June picked it up and took it to the sunlight slanting in from a port-hole.

And stared.

What the fuck IS it?

It was a six or seven-inch long metallic object with rounded edges and a not-quite-symmetrical contour. The only thing she could think to compare it to would be a Baby Ruth bar, but of course Baby Ruth bars were not made of solid gold.

This thing was.

It's a gold ingot or something! June deduced. *That old fuck Kupjack really DID find gold!*

June's heart pattered. She paced back and forth, wide-eyed. This thing in her hand was obviously only a tiny bit of the entire stash Kupjack had found. *Like when you bite into a sandwich and a crumb falls to the floor,* came a weighty simile. And with the price of gold over a thousand dollar an ounce, here was the nest egg poor June had never gotten even after a life of hard, honest work. And she knew one thing for sure: *This fuckin' Baby Ruth bar is coming home with ME.*

Stealing, schmeeling. It wasn't hers, no, but Finder's Keepers. *Kupjack has ENOUGH gold and he sure as shit knows where there's more. So...fuck him.* She put the gold bar/piece/ingot/whatever it was in her pocket. But, even though she now possessed a small fortune, she'd still have to paint the damn boat or else Kupjack would be suspicious. The piece in her pocket he'd dropped unnoticed, but if she quit on the spot—

He'll know I found something.

Therefore, she resolved to get to work and make it seem that everything was normal, yet as she prepared to retrieve the dropcloths, rollers, etc., the most natural thought occurred to her:

Maybe there's more. Maybe there are a few more pieces lying around that Kupjack dropped and didn't notice!

Some inner-monitor went off in her brain which said, *You've got enough. Don't be greedy,* and to this monitor she promptly replied, *Fuck off.*

On hands and knees, she proceeded, patting the ancient floor in every dark corner, and it must be said that the excitement derived from finding a chunk of pure gold combined with the excitement of possibly finding more.... June was not surprised to find the "purse of her loins" beating like a heart and drenching her crotch; and though her mind was quite set on gold, part of her cognizance was overwhelmed by imagery of the most lusty sort: dicks in her mouth, dicks in her butt, dicks in her "honey bucket." All these things and more poured over her mind's eye, and one imaginary cock after another dumped great plumes of sperm in her and on her. June was so horny, as a matter of fact, that she had to force herself *not* to stick her hand down her shorts for some stimulation of a more substantial nature. *Masturbate later, you horn dog! Right now you're looking for gold!*

But, lo, in her extensive, knee-dirtying search, no gold was to be found. However she *did* discover one beer cap, a cigar butt, an M&M (a green one), and—

Yuck!

87

–a rubber glove with brown index finger. It was clear how the good Captain Kupjack utilized his spare time.

She moved on, next, to a tiny storage closet, which she felt inclined to skip but for some reason didn't.

Perhaps she should have.

She unlatched the narrow door, and—

Holy motherfucking FUCK!

–out spilled a veritable *pile* of skeletons. Easily the bones of four men were in evidence, and she didn't need to be scholar of Euclidean calculus to realize that the bones constituted Kupjack's "crew." June naturally ejected herself from the compartment in a split-second, but a split-second was enough to digest the horror's details.

The skeletons still had their clothes on, the fabric of which seemed half corroded. One would think that the men had rotted down to bare bones while the clothing remained, but how could this be? There was no stench of death at all, if anything just a pleasant sea-scent. The eye-socket of one victim remained filled by a glass eye. This could only be Tommy Ray Swain, a local deadbeat fishing hand who liked to pop the eye out at the bar and put in people's drinks, not an activity which was met with any levity. June had fucked him once in high school but wished she hadn't. For one thing, she'd received no orgasm for her efforts, for another, she got a UTI.

But that was another story.

The bones were clean, too, scrapless. Not a single sinew of flesh, tendon, or cartilage could be found on any of them.

Be that as it may, June ran her 90-pound ass out of there as fast as her coltish legs could carry her. She tore across the main cabin, shot herself up the companionway steps, grabbed the door latch, and–

Fuck fuck fuck fuck fuck fuck FUCK!

The door was locked!

It must've locked by itself when she'd come down. She

kicked at it ferociously. It didn't budge. Then...

What the FUCK?!

And errant glance out porthole on the door showed her this:

Good ole Kupjack sitting in the captain's chair in the wheelhouse, swigging a bottle of Wild Turkey.

How could he not have heard me kicking the door, the old fuck? And with that thought, June POUNDED on the door with all her might. "Hey!" she shrieked. "I locked myself in! Open the door!"

Kupjack made no motion, no response.

And only then did June realize that the door *couldn't* be locked accidentally from the outside. It was a deadbolt which required a key...

"YOU FAT DRUNK PERVERT MOTHERFUCKER!" she bellowed. "YOU LOCKED ME IN!"

At this, Kupjack turned around in the chair, faced the outside of the door, and waved, grinning, right at June.

Whatever was going on here, June hadn't time to conjecture but she instantaneously knew three things.

One, there was no breaking through the door without an ax.

Two, there was an ax in the engine room.

Three, to get to the engine room, she'd have to pass the skeleton pile at the closet, and there was a formidable probability that on such a trek, she would encounter whatever it was that had sucked the flesh off the bodies of four men.

Oh, and Four, the only reason Kupjack would've locked her inside was because he must strongly desire June meet the same fate as his crew.

June's teeth chattered as she daintily stepped over the tumble of corpses that had spilled into the narrow hall. To get to the engine room, she'd have to first pass through the bunk cabin, and this she did with some trepidation–so much trepidation, in fact, that she wet herself. *Terrific,* she thought.

It was dark here, only one round window deck level on each side, and, wouldn't she know it, the light switch was on the other side of the cabin, next to the engine room door. Stifling heat seemed to pressure-cook her; she was pouring sweat. Not three steps across the floor and she felt the oddest bumps under her flipflops, as if she were walking over pebbles. When she looked down, even in the limited light, she saw that the "pebbles" were marble-sized nuggets of gold.

She noticed something else as well: a creeky low-tide scent. The cabin was only six feet long, but it felt like six hundred. Six bunks, three on each side, lined the walls, and in the occluded light, crumpled sheets and pillows looked like men. June didn't need that illusion. Then again—

What's that smell?

It was earthy, musky without being unwholesome, and, truth be told, it was kind of a turn on.

"This is NOT the best time to be horny!" she whispered to herself.

At last she made it to the door to the engine room, grabbed the latch, turned it, and–

Oh, for dick's sake!

–it was locked.

No recourse now but to return to the main door at the top of the companionway steps. And–*The fire extinguisher!* There was one on the wall. *Maybe I can break the door down with that!*

Just as she would open the door that led out of the bunk cabin–

click

–someone locked it from the other side.

Bugged-eyed, June looked through the little round window and saw Kupjack smiling at her.

She bellowed loud as a trumpet: "You drunk old fat perverted piece of dog shit! Unlock the door! What's going on? What did you do to your crew? I'll KILL YA when I get out of here!"

She could just hear his voice, muffled as it was, through the door, "You WON'T get out of there, sweetie"–then he cackled a laugh. "Look up at the ceiling."

The ceiling? June was stifled, her mind a mix of terror and questions. She looked up at the ceiling and saw nothing of note at first; there wasn't enough light to see anything but the fact that the ceiling was black, or almost black. But as she squinted at an irregularity, her eyes began to acclimate to the low light, and in the corner of her eye, she noticed, right there on a bunk (next to a magazine entitled *All Hands On Dick!* and a jar of vaseline), a large flashlight.

Fuck yeah! came the cultured thought, and she grabbed the flashlight, snapped it on and pointed the strong beam of light toward the ceiling....

And peed in her shorts again.

The ceiling...was *moving.*

Think of a 300-pound blob of fresh-made bread dough dropped on the floor, and the way it would slowly spread outward. That's what this reminded June of, only it wasn't on the floor, it was on the fucking ceiling, and this wasn't bread dough, because bread dough wasn't the color of, well, feces.

Then the blob detached itself from the ceiling and fell right on June.

Holy motherfucking SHIT! she thought, struggling at once with the tent of churning slop that had landed on her. It formed something like a bubble over her, whose confines were very slowly drawing in, and June received the strangest impression that the, the, the *thing* was doing this on purpose, to lengthen the time of her terror before it had entirely converged on her. She received several more strong impressions as well, and another was that the mass of surf-smelling poop-brown glop had every intention of eating her.

Whatever the thing was, June didn't care. An alien that

had landed in the sea? A secret genetic experiment run amok? Or just some unclassified, previously undiscovered sea-creature?

June didn't give a flying fuck.

She collapsed down on her back, then stuck her legs out straight–a feeble attempt, at least, to put struts between herself and that ever-lowering mass of sea-blubber, excrescence, reef-slop, or whatever it was. The flashlight remained on, and as the top of that "bubble" sunk around her feet, she pointed the light upwards.

I'm WAY out of my league here, she thought quite dismally, and she peed her pants again, too, by the way. Puckered holes began to emerge from the slop's inner-surface area, like octopus suckers, and all at once, she deduced what had happened to the crew. Once these suckers made contact with her flesh, they would emit slimy digestive enzymes and then they would, well, they would *suck.* They would suck all her flesh off her bones. And once she'd been liquified and digested, any moron knew what happened next. What goes in, must come out, right? June would be processed through the creature's bowels and then excreted through whatever manner of monster-anus this hideous thing had in its butt.

More than that, she would be excreted, not as common poop, but as *gold.*

It began to occur to her, as her feet struggled against the descending wet mass, that she knew far too much than she had any business knowing. These rapid impressions that fired into her mind had no logical explanation, but still the impressions came, and with them the full gist. *This fuckin' ugly pile of shit is TELEPATHIC!* she realized. *It's sending signals to my brain and letting me know all about it!*

Ever-so-slowly, it continued to constrict, those suckers throbbing. Using her legs as struts against the top of the "bubble" did no good at all. Just as she *knew* the mass would collapse on her and begin to chow down, she noticed the strangest thing in the shifting illumination of the flashlight...

A cock and balls.

Or something *like* a cock and balls: a glistening milk-chocolate-brown sack heavy with two fist-sized lumps semblant of testicles, over which lay what could only be a flaccid, veined, uncircumcised *sea-peter.*

June's sentience shifted into a thoughtless, almost automatic mode. She did not consciously *think,* she merely *acted* the only way her instincts knew.

She shot her hand out, and began to fondle the bizarre genitals.

Her fingers played with the testicles for a few moments; she could feel them beating from within, and as she did so, she noticed something of significance:

The entirety of the mass of slop which surrounded her *stopped* descending.

I'll bet the fucker's horny, she deduced. *Probably hasn't a piece of sea-slug ass in a long time. Let's see how he likes a HUMAN piece of ass...*

She kneed her way through dripping ichor, and with no hesitation whatsoever she pulled what could only be the thing's penis into her mouth, all the while maintaining her titillation of its lumpen gonads. The penis did not come erect as a human one would but instead throbbed in her mouth like an animate pile of wet modeling clay. June's tongue roved over it, feeling the fascinating network of beating veins, and once or twice sliding over the meaty, rimmed aperture which she could only guess was the end of its urethra. An inclination directed her to try pushing her entire tongue *into* that aperture, and when it dilated enough for her to do so, she knew she'd made the right choice. The creature actually *shuddered* in pleasure.

And still, the body of the thing did not collapse on her and subsequently consume her. *It wants a blowjob,* she realized. *Gee, why is THAT no surprise?* But this thing's cock was so different from a man's, she wasn't sure how to commence. While weighing considerations, she "fucked" the monster's peehole with her tongue, plunging in and out, and figured the sensation was lengthening her life. The peehole, however, constricted after another minute, and June figured that meant it was time to get down to business. She began to tighten her mouth around the veined wad of flesh but it was too wide for her to rim her lips around as she would a regular dick. But then?

Yowza!

The odd penile mass in her mouth suddenly protracted, narrowing by degrees, and advanced down her throat. This advancement did not abate until it reached her stomach. It was June's good fortune that she possessed no gag-reflex. The situation could be likened to, say, a girthy snake slithering down from her mouth into her belly.

Here goes nothing...

She began to move her head back and forth, the action of which caused her throat to slide to and fro over every inch of that "snake." *Fuck!* she thought. *This isn't deep throat, this is deep stomach!* She could feel the thing tensing, and she sensed in a more psychical way that the creature was going ga-ga over her oral ministration. But evidently, dicks were universal: if you suck one, it blows its load, and so was the case with *this* dick at that very moment.

June's eyeballs nearly started from her head. The thing came in her stomach as though it were a manual feeding tube. *You gotta be shitting me!* Was it a pint? A quart? June's belly filled with hot slop, and when the snake-like penile shaft withdrew from her throat, it was *still* coming. Quart, be damned—this thing was working on a gallon! Upon full withdrawal, her mouth filled with its cum as well.

What was the creature's sperm *like?*

Hot Tapioca pudding? A bucket of shucked raw oysters? A colossal volume of frog eggs? All these similes combined would probably be a just parallel. The amount of it in her stomach was a grim prospect indeed; it seemed to bubble down there, and shift, and percolate. *At least I don't have to worry about buying dinner...* Further considerations bewildered her. For one, after being orally pummeled by a sea-monster's cock, she would expect herself to be repulsed and terrified, not—

Not *what?*

Horny, she realized.

June was horny, all right, hornier than a nun full of Spanish Fly. Her vagina beat like a angry fist banging against a door. She gave up trying to isolate her thoughts when she realized that the *thing's* thoughts were still seeping into her head, but in no language but that of raw emotion: lust, desire, need, and, yes, love!

This great big plop of monster-slime LOVES ME!

And in a moment more, June—with no conscious forethought whatsoever–physically availed herself to *receive* the sea-monster's love. She was out of her shorts, and spread-eagled on her back in less time than it took to say *Fuck the shit out of me!* It was during these few seconds before physical intercourse would ensue that the same *mental/psychic* intercourse became more acute. *Yeah, this thing loves me, all right, and it's about to prove that in spades,* June thought but, by now she was ready for some love herself, some *hard* love. Her feminine channel was drenched, her nipples gorged to a size she'd never before experienced, tingling electrically and actually throbbing. Her loins felt like a pot of Sex Stew, bubbling, roiling, cringing to be stirred, and she knew that she was undergoing some serious hormonal or cerbro-chemical change. Was it normal to *want* to be fucked by a sea-monster? Meanwhile, the sea-monster underwent a change of its own. That massive "bubble"-shape of its body began to turn inside-out and backwards, and when this prolapsation had finished, there stood before

June some 300 pounds of brown, mottled, low-tide-smelling porridge which bore the most vague semblance of the human form: i.e.: jointless, digitless arms and legs, an undetailed approximation of a trunk, an eyeless, noseless, mouthless earless lump for a head. Think a monstrous gingerbread man, or a shit-colored Gumby doll...

However, Gumby was not possessed of erection, but this thing was, sticking up like a foot-and-a-half-inch length of veined, pulsing radiator hose. Precum ran like a leaky tap from the puckered slit which crowned the glans. Those same malformed, fist-sized testicles to which June had been previously introduced, constricted in their hideous scrotum even as June stared up, drooling, legs spread painfully apart; and somehow, in the most abstract and introspective insinuation, the monster stared back at her with equal desire in spite of the fact no eyes could be found in its lumpen head.

In a sense of need which could only be likened to insanity, June's hands plied her gushing sex, the sensations of which she had never felt with such potency. *If this thing doesn't start banging the daylights out of my RIGHT NOW, I'm gonna have to fist myself!*

"Come on, pal!" she bellowed. "Let me have it!" She lewdly thrust her splayed groin forward. "Does it look like you need a fucking invitation?"

We need not accompany June through the preambles which led up to the business at hand; it should suffice to say, instead, that in a hackneyed wink of an eye, that man-shaped heap of ocean-slop landed on her with the urgency of a pit bull on a meat wagon. June wanted to get fucked, and fucked she got. The thing made mewling sounds as it lay atop her, humping away, drawing that malleable cock in and out of June's "love-hole." Just as it had lengthened and narrowed in order to advance into her belly, it now lengthened and narrowed to advance into deepest depths of her reproductive tract. At the front of her cervix, it seemed to turn semi-solid and then poured farther, farther, deeper, deeper, through the physical limits of the uterus, then impossibly dividing into two squirming tendrils, each of which quivered still deeper up into the fallopian tubes. The spasms of sensation that coursed through June's body were clearly sensations hitherto unfelt before by any human woman. The thing continued to hump her without relent, all the while those delectable "dick-tendrils" continued to quiver and elicit neural pleasures so intense that all June could do was lie there–drooling, tongue out, limp-limbed–and *feel.* The sentient part of her brain shut off so that it might focus solely on the waves of orgasms that pulsed through her being. Eventually her musky lover's orgasm commenced as well, triggered by the release of its pudding-like sperm: gushes of it, which blew against every inner recess of June's reproductive apparatus. When the thing clumsily began to get up, the unearthly penis continued to pour still more sperm into her, and when that was done, it stood upright and looked sightlessly down at June, whose body just went on spasming in orgasm for at least another half hour.

***

Captain Kupjack sat above deck under the wheelhouse awning, nearly done with his first bottle of Wild Turkey for the day. A smile of robust satisfaction touched the booze-reddened face, and in further satisfaction he even gave his crotch a squeeze. The idea simply tickled him pink: June being consumed, digested, and pushed out of that hideous thing's butthole. *That smartass cunt finally gets what she deserves,* his thoughts cackled. She'd sassed him for years, and smirked off every advance, even turned down his offers of good money, while fucking and sucking every cock in town, every cock but poor old Captain Kupjack's. *Too good for me, huh, tramp? Think you're too high-falutin'for the*

Captain, huh? Well, how do ya like me now?

Now?

By now that redneck gravyboat is nothing but a pile of solid-gold shit on the floor.

Yes, Kupjack liked that idea very much.

He waited a while longer, idly stroking his beard and giving further errant squeezes to his groin, until the sun pulled off a bit more, and then he got up and creaked his wobbling fat frame down the steps to the lower deck. When he arrived at the engine room door, he smiled into the porthole, looking for the telltale skeleton which would be all that remained of that fickle white-trash sperm depository named June. However–

"Where the hell is she?"

No evidence of June's remains were to be seen, and only then did the Captain notice that the door was no longer locked and that the deadbolt had been broken *outward.*

What kind'a monkeyshines goin' on here? he thought and scratched his Amish-style beard, and then he thought that maybe things had not gone as he'd planned and that maybe he should shag his fat drunken ass the fuck out of there without delay, but–

"Looking for someone?" a snide voice issued behind him.

It took a moment for the implication to register through Kupjack's whiskey-fogged perceptions as he turned, squinting, and saw none other than June herself standing behind him, buck naked and sheened in perspiration. "Why, ya conniving jizz-head whore! That thing should'a et ya by now!"

"It was going to," June replied, "until I fucked and sucked it to kingdom come and it fell in love with me." She looked up to the ceiling. "Honey? Be a sweetheart and come down here. You must be real hungry after all that wonderful lovin' you gave me. Well, soup's on!"

Kupjack was already screaming as the sea-slop slithered down the wall and engulfed him. June used a nearby bunk for a ringside seat; the only thing missing was popcorn. The Captain's pathetic fat form could be seen struggling uselessly within the churning, ravenous pile. She had to credit the old perv at least in his resolve to garble every possible sexist expletive at her for as long as his vocal cords functioned. We need not repeat those expletives here...well, on second thought, maybe we will, just a few, in the interests of completeness:

"Ya dirty white-trash cutthroat fuck-toilet!"

"Low-down tramp, done chugged more cock than I've chugged whiskey!"

"Bet you've had more dick going *into* your ass than shit comin' *out!*"

And so on. At any rate, that was the end of Captain Kupjack, and the beginning of a new life for June!

***

A week later, June stretched out in a lounge chair on the sundeck of her brand-new 72-foot Stardust houseboat. No more shitty efficiency apartment for her, and no more minimum-wage jobs busting her tail for asshole sexual-predator bosses. Nope, it was the high-life for June from now on. In the trunk of Kupjack's Cadillac (which June had ransacked the night of the Captain's "disappearance") she'd found several million in gold turds, not to mention the additional gold that the man had been turned into by the sea-slug's digestive tract. She'd never have to lift a finger again in her life, and she figured she deserved it.

"Rummy, get me another Long Island Iced Tea, will you?" came her languid request from the lounge chair. It was great to just lay around all day on the boat, soaking up the sun and getting loaded. She'd hired Rummy and Fishy as her crew–why not? They were shiftless alcoholic idiots but she figured they deserved a break. They waited on her hand and foot, cleaned the boat, cooked her meals, etc. June liked the idea of being waited on by men.

"Comin' right up!" Rummy replied after having just finished peeing over the side. Then he shuffled off to the galley where there was a fully stocked bar. Fishy was down below in the back, scraping barnacles off the prop, and June simply continued to lie there, in her Bill Blass bikini, her Ray-ban sunglasses, and a $300 Tropicana sun hat, and she would be happy to spend the rest of her days just like this. *Ah, the good life!* she thought.

But one question remained, did it not?

Whatever happened to the sea-slop thing?

Tempted as she was to keep it locked up for use as her personal sex minister, she knew that would be terribly cruel. It was a creature of the wild and an inhabitant of the deep blue sea–what*ever* the fuck it was–so in the deep blue sea it belonged.

And into the deep blue sea, she released it.

The best piece of male ass I ever had, she lamented, because she would've been perfectly content to let it fuck the stuffing out of her every day for the rest of her life. But how fair would that be to...to...*it?* To the sea-thing, the sea-monster, the...whatever the fuck it was?

This she knew beyond all doubt: no human man would ever be good enough ever again. But there was also something else she knew with equal certainty:

I was the best fuck of that thing's life.

She gazed out into the endless sea and smiled. See, that abstruse psychic connection she and it had shared never really severed with its departure. And June knew full well that that great big wonderful pile of sea-slop would be stopping by very soon for a booty call.

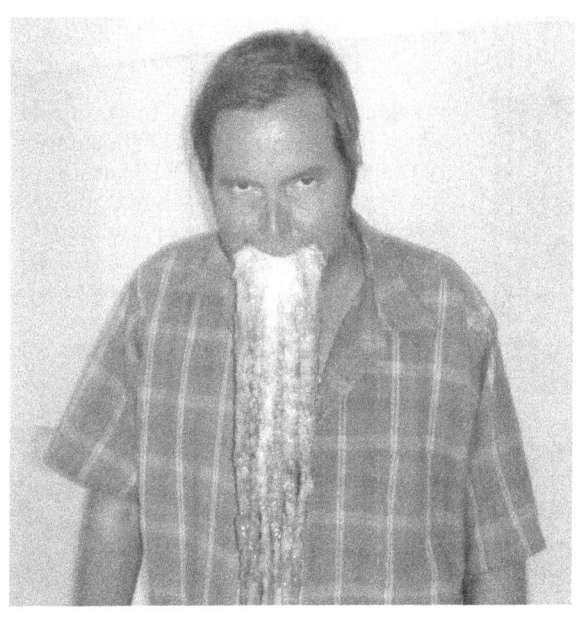

ABOUT THE AUTHOR

Edward Lee has authored close to 50 books in the
field of horror; he specializes in hardcore fare. His
most recent novels are LUCIFER'S LOTTERY
and the Lovecraftian THE HAUNTER OF THE
THRESHOLD. His movie HEADER was released
on DVD by Synapse Film in June, 2009. Lee lives
in Largo, Florida.

deadite press

"Header" Edward Lee - In the dark backwoods, where law enforcement doesn't dare tread, there exists a special type of revenge. Something so awful that it is only whispered about. Something so terrible that few believe it is real. Stewart Cummings is a government agent whose life is going to Hell. His wife is ill and to pay for her medication he turns to bootlegging. But things will get much worse when bodies begin showing up in his sleepy small town. Victims of an act known only as "a Header."

"Entombed II" Brian Keene- It has been several months since the disease known as Hamelin's Revenge decimated the world. Civilization has collapsed and the dead far outnumber the living. The survivors seek refuge from the roaming zombie hordes, but one-by-one, those shelters are falling. Twenty-five survivors barricade themselves inside a former military bunker buried deep beneath a luxury hotel. They are safe from the zombies...but are they safe from one another?

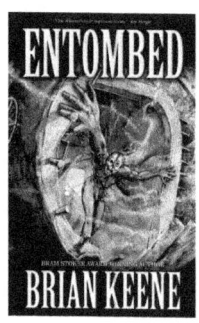

"Zombies and Shit" Carlton Mellick III - Twenty people wake to find themselves in a boarded-up building in the middle of the zombie wasteland. They soon discover they have been chosen as contestants on a popular reality show called Zombie Survival. Each contestant is given a backpack of supplies and a unique weapon. Their goal: be the first to make it through the zombie-plagued city to the pick-up zone alive. But because there's only one seat available on the helicopter, the contestants not only have to fight against the hordes of the living dead, they must also fight each other.

"Muerte Con Carne" Shane McKenzie - Human flesh tacos, hardcore wrestling, and angry cannibal Mexicans, Welcome to the Border! Felix and Marta came to Mexico to film a documentary on illegal immigration. When Marta suddenly goes missing, Felix must find his lost love in the small border town. A dangerous place housing corrupt cops, borderline maniacs, and something much more worse than drug gangs, something to do with a strange Mexican food cart...

deadite press

"Urban Gothic" Brian Keene - When their car broke down in a dangerous inner-city neighborhood, Kerri and her friends thought they would find shelter inside an old, dark row home. They thought they would be safe there until help arrived. They were wrong. The residents who live down in the cellar and the tunnels beneath the city are far more dangerous than the streets outside, and they have a very special way of dealing with trespassers. Trapped in a world of darkness, populated by obscene abominations, they will have to fight back if they ever want to see the sun again.

"Ghoul" Brian Keene - There is something in the local cemetery that comes out at night. Something that is unearthing corpses and killing people. It's the summer of 1984 and Timmy and his friends are looking forward to no school, comic books, and adventure. But instead they will be fighting for their lives. The ghoul has smelled their blood and it is after them. But that's not the only monster they will face this summer . . . From award-winning horror master Brian Keene comes a novel of monsters, murder, and the loss of innocence.

"Clickers" J. F. Gonzalez and Mark Williams- They are the Clickers, giant venomous blood-thirsty crabs from the depths of the sea. The only warning to their rampage of dismemberment and death is the terrible clicking of their claws. But these monsters aren't merely here to ravage and pillage. They are being driven onto land by fear. Something is hunting the Clickers. Something ancient and without mercy. *Clickers* is J. F. Gonzalez and Mark Williams' gore-soaked cult classic tribute to the giant monster B-movies of yesteryear.

"Clickers II" J. F. Gonzalez and Brian Keene- Thousands of Clickers swarm across the entire nation and march inland, slaughtering anyone and anything they come across. But this time the Clickers aren't blindly rushing onto land - they are being led by an intelligence older than civilization itself. A force that wants to take dry land away from the mammals. Those left alive soon realize that they must do everything and anything they can to protect humanity – no matter the cost. *This isn't war, this is extermination.*

"The Book of a Thousand Sins" Wrath James White - Welcome to a world of Zombie nymphomaniacs, psychopathic deities, voodoo surgery, and murderous priests. Where mutilation sex clubs are in vogue and torture machines are sex toys. No one makes it out alive – not even God himself.
"If Wrath James White doesn't make you cringe, you must be riding in the wrong end of a hearse."
    -Jack Ketchum

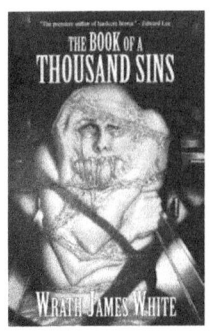

"Whargoul" Dave Brockie - It is a beast born in bullets and shrapnel, feeding off of pain, misery, and hard drugs. Cursed to wander the Earth without the hope of death, it is reborn again and again to spread the gospel of hate, abuse, and genocide. But what if it's not the only monster out there? What if there's something worse? From Dave Brockie, the twisted genius behind GWAR, comes a novel about the darkest days of the twentieth century.

"Take the Long Way Home" Brian Keene - All across the world, people suddenly vanish in the blink of an eye. Gone. Steve, Charlie and Frank were just trying to get home when it happened. Trapped in the ultimate traffic jam, they watch as civilization collapses, claiming the souls of those around them. God has called his faithful home, but the invitations for Steve, Charlie and Frank got lost. Now they must set off on foot through a nightmarish post-apocalyptic landscape in search of answers. In search of God. In search of their loved ones. And in search of home.

"Baby's First Book of Seriously Fucked-Up Shit" Robert Devereaux - From an orgy between God, Satan, Adam and Eve to beauty pageants for fetuses. From a giant human-absorbing tongue to a place where God is in the eyes of the psychopathic. This is a party at the furthest limits of human decency and cruelty. Robert Devereaux is your host but watch out, he's spiked the punch with drugs, sex, and dismemberment. Deadite Press is proud to present nine stories of the strange, the gross, and the just plain fucked up.

THE VERY BEST IN CULT HORROR

www.ingramcontent.com/pod-product-compliance
Lightning Source LLC
Chambersburg PA
CBHW060132260626

47160CB00005B/2080